Philip Slaughter, Henry Fry

Memoir of Col. Joshua Fry

Philip Slaughter, Henry Fry

Memoir of Col. Joshua Fry

ISBN/EAN: 9783337274733

Printed in Europe, USA, Canada, Australia, Japan

Cover: Foto ©Raphael Reischuk / pixelio.de

More available books at **www.hansebooks.com**

MEMOIR

OF

COL. JOSHUA FRY,

SOMETIME

Professor in William and Mary College, Virginia,

AND

WASHINGTON'S SENIOR IN COMMAND OF VIRGINIA
FORCES, 1754, ETC., ETC.,

WITH AN

AUTOBIOGRAPHY OF HIS SON,

REV. HENRY FRY,

AND A

CENSUS OF THEIR DESCENDANTS,

BY THE

REV. P. SLAUGHTER, D. D.,

AUTHOR OF

"HISTORY OF ST. GEORGE'S PARISH," "ST. MARK'S
PARISH," "BRISTOL PARISH," ETC., ETC.

CONTENTS OF THE MEMOIR.

INTRODUCTION; RADIATION OF COUNTIES FROM THEIR ORIGINAL CENTRES.

CHAPTER I.

CHAPTER II.

4

Howard, Major; Wm. Randolph, Sheriff; Dr. Wm. Cabell, Thos. Turpin, Thos. Bellew, Assistant Surveyors; Sketch of the Cabells; Hugh Blair Grigsby, L.L.D.; County Court system, Dr. Wm. P. Palmer; Madam Mary Fry; papers of Rev. Rt. Rose and Patrick Henry; Alexander Brown, of Union Hill.

CHAPTER III.

Northern Neck of Va.; Lord Fairfax, Proprietor, Limits of his Patent, etc.; Commissioners for running the line (1736); Col. Wm. Byrd, Jno. Grymes and Jno. Robinson, for the Crown, and Wm. Fairfax, Wm. Beverdey, and Chas. Carter, for Lord Fairfax; New Commission (1745) Col. Fry, Col. Lunsford and Major P. Hedgeman, for the Crown; line marked from Head Spring of Conway River to Head Spring of Potomac; Chas. Jas. Faulkner's Report; valuable documents referred to by him, stolen from State Library during the Federal occupation of Richmond.

CHAPTER IV.

Boundary line between Virginia and North Carolina, run from the sea to Peters' Creek, (1728) by Col. Wm. Byrd, Richard Fitzwilliam and Wm. Dandridge; Continued by Fry and Jefferson, (1749); completed by Dr. Thos. Walker and David Smith, (1778).

CHAPTER V.

Colonial Maps of Virginia; Capt. Jno. Smith's, Herman's, Mitchell's, Mayo's, Fry and Jefferson's, Henry's, etc.; Wm. Green, L.L.D.; Joseph Horner, Antiquary.

CHAPTER VI.

CHAPTER VII.

CHAPTER VIII.

GENEALOGY.

Census of the Descendants of Col. Fry and Mary
(Micou) Fry, and of their intermarriages with the
Walkers,. Maurys, Adams, Harrisons, Smiths, Coxs,
Montgomerys, Barbees, Winstons, Greens, Beattys,
Johnstons, Borsleys, Bells, Bullitts, Marshalls, Hen-
rys, Speeds, Henrys, Logans, Langhores, Hennings,
Keats, Coles, Chenowiths. Dixons, Stiles, Burbanks,
Fredericks, Breckenridges, Peays, Tuleys, Rodgers,
McDonalds, Crutchers, Menifees, Phillips, Hardys.
Hewitts, Lightfoots, Visschers, Nashs, Chipmans,
Ingersolls, Gardettes, Berkleys, Childs, Patriarchs,
Jones, ˈ Hendees, Harveys, Hopes, McCulloughs,
Hallidays, Hugans, Paynes, Maupins, Mortons, Craw-
fords, Doyles, Simpsons, Nounnans, Harmers, Mc-
Lanes, Ruffners, Taylors, Wilsons, Pauls, Edgars,
McIlhannys, Mathews, Hoffnagles, Donnellys, Gosh-
horns, Allens, Andersons, Odens, Shorters, Davis,
Whites, Hutchins, Humes, Bacons, Boykins, Spen-
cers, Mayers, Pattersons, Franklins, Fielders, Crit-
tendens, Herndons, Chapins, Conners, Turners,
Hudgins, Yanceys, Clarkes, Edges, Sparks, Garnetts.
Thomas, Watsons, Lewis, Barksdales, Dunkums,
Mitchells, Shepherds, Millers, Willis, Rankins, Mc-
Laurins, Starrs, Heiskells, Goodmans, Davidsons,
Haywoods, Minors, Bentons, Banks, Browns, Hob-
sons, Carsons, Ruckers, Aylers, Hills, Bookers,
Daniels, Webbs, Burnetts, Nichols, Sturgis, Brad-

fords, Divers, Leighs, Leflets, Carpenters, Saunders, Winns, Nicholas, Taliaferros, Thompsons, Carters, Scotts, Slaughters, etc.

FAMILY OF DR. THOMAS WALKER, OF CASTLE HILL.

Their intermarriages with Merewethers, Thorntons, Moores, Frys, Maurys, Lewis, Lindsays, Dukes, Rives, Pages, Nelsons, Dr. Geo. Gilmer, Frank Gilmer, (Professor) Thos. Walker Gilmer, Governor and Secretary of War; Wm. Wirt, Attorney General, etc.

FAMILY OF HON. WM. CABELL RIVES.

Tablet to his memory in Grace Church, Walker's Parish; intermarriages of his children with the Barclays, Sears, Sigourneys, and McMurdos.

Supplement to Walker's and Merewether's.

REV. JAMES MAURY.

His credentials from Commissary Blair, of Virginia, to the Bishop of London, Rev. Matthew Maury; Capt. Matthew Fontaine Maury; his extraordinary career; enumeration of the honors conferred upon him by the crowned heads and by Scientific Societies, etc., of Europe; Baron Von Humboldt, etc.

Record in Family Bible of Col. Fielding Lewis, of Fredericksburg; Names of his Children, and of the God-fathers and God-mothers of each of them, including Gen. Washington, Mrs. Mary Washington, Mrs. Martha Washington, Samuel Washington, Col. Francis Thornton, and his brothers John and George, etc., etc.

Major Byrd C. Willis, of Willis Hill.

His family reminiscences; Col. Henry Willis and Mrs. Gregory; Gen. Washington at School; Achille Murat, etc., etc.; Col. George Willis, of Wood Park, etc.

Nicholas Family.

Dr. George Nicholas, the first of the name in Virginia; Rt. Carter Nicholas, Wilson Cary Nicholas, Philip Norlorne Nicholas; their intermarriages with the Carters, Carys, Randolphs, Taylors, Byrds, Nortons, Frys, etc.

INDEX TO THE AUTO-BIOGRAPHY OF THE REV. HENRY FRY.

Introduction; the Author's reasons for editing it; Methodist Preacher in Paris, (France); H. Fry's birth; his youth in Williamsburg; removal to Albemarle; Deputy to Jno. C. Nicholas; Clerk; his marriage; his removal to Culpeper; his conversion; graphic picture of his passage from darkness to light; good humored debates with his Baptist neighbors; interviews with their preachers, Eve, Waller, T. A.; first hearing of, and meeting with the Methodists; conference at Manakin Town; Methodist Preachers, — Williams, Pride, Gatch, Little-John, Drumgoole and Coke; becomes a Class-Leader and Exhorter; surprised into preaching; represents Culpeper in Legislature; curious account of his reception in Richmond and intercourse with members of Assembly; Assessment Bill; Emancipation Bill; return home and illness; anecdote of Elder James Garnett in his chamber; Col. Taylor's Diary; preaches in Brick Church (Episcopal) in Orange, alternately with Waddell (Presbyterian), and Bellmaine and Maury (Episcopal) ministers; preaches Col. Charles Porter's funeral (with Tatum).

William Wirt makes Mr. Fry's house his home for several years; his fondness for fishing and writing comedies; begins practice of Law; his office near Locust Dale; relics of it; original letters from Thos. Jefferson, President, to Mr. Fry, about Priestley's

Works, and the medical uses of long journeys on horseback, etc.; Wesley Fry with Wirt, when he heard Waddell preach, etc.; Mr. Fry attends Bishop Moore's first Episcopal visit to Culpeper, to witness the Confirmation of his Daughter-in-Law; his pleasure on the occasion; the Death of his Wife; the breaking up of his home and his removal to his son Wesley's; his increasing infirmities and peaceful death; his Obituary.

INTRODUCTION TO THE MEMOIRS.

RADIATION OF COUNTIES FROM THEIR ORIGINAL CENTRES.

This memoir and the history of persons and places in Virginia, generally, will be better understood, if readers would observe the radiation of counties from their original centres, viz. : the eight primitive shires into which the Colony was divided in 1634 ; not (as is currently said) by the House of Burgesses, but more probably, if not certainly, by the Governor and Council, in obedience to instructions repeatedly given by the Crown, before that date. The Counties on James River, from James City to Albemarle, comprehended both sides of the river, until Surry was taken from the South side, (1652) ; Prince George from Charles City, (1702) ; Chesterfield from Henrico, (1748). When Goochland was created out of the North side of Henrico (1727), it embraced both sides of the river, until Cumberland was cut out of its South side, (1748). When Albemarle was formed from Goochland, (1744), it crossed the river, until Buckingham was taken out of its South side, (1761). Amherst, formed in the same year from Albemarle, did not cross the river, because Bedford was already there, having been propagated along another line, from

Surry, through Prince George, Brunswick and Lun-
enburg, from which last, Bedford sprang in 1753.
Campbell was taken from Bedford in 1784, and Nelson from Amherst in 1807. When Old Albemarle
(1744), reached the Blue Ridge, it met Augusta,
which had come by another line from the primitive
Shire, York. Thus, New Kent, King and Queen,
King William, Essex, Spotsylvania, Orange, Augusta.
New Kent had thrown off Hanover, which ended in
Louisa. Orange had thrown off Culpeper, which
ended in Madison and Rappahannock ; and also,
Frederick, which became another centre of radiation,
etc. It is well to say, too, that James River, above
the mouth of the Rivanna, is called in this Memoir,
the "Fluvanna," by which name it was then known,
and is called in Acts of Assembly to 1806, at least ;
(see Shepherd, v. 3, p. 333). Albemarle, in history,
is said to have been taken wholly out of Goochland ;
but an Act of Assembly (8 Henning, p. 54) affirms
that its Northern Section was once in Hanover, which
happened thus : When Louisa was taken from Hanover it contained this Northern Section, but when
Amherst was taken from Albemarle, compensation
was made, by adding the said section of Louisa

NOTE.—The orthography of rivers and places varies in different documents.
For example : the Robinson River is often printed Robertson. On Mayo's
map (1736), it is thus called. On Fry's map (1749), it is Robinson, and also
in Henning's Statutes. There was a Dr. Robinson and a Col. Robertson with
Governor Spotswood when the head-waters of the Rapid Ann were explored ;
and after one of these, this river may have been named. See "St. Mark's
Parish," Chapter, "Knight's of the Horse Shoe."

to Albemarle. Attention to these details will explain seeming discrepancies arising out of the fact that settlers on the frontiers found themselves citizens of several counties in succession, without changing their abodes. The same person, in the same place, may have been a citizen of Henrico, of Goochland, of Albemarle, and of Amherst.

MEMOIR OF COL. JOSHUA FRY.

CHAPTER I.

At the junction of the Robinson River and what, in old times, was called the Meander,* but is now known by the more prosaic name of Crooked Run, lies one of the best farms in Piedmontese Virginia. It was patented in 1726–39 by Joshua Fry, the root in Virginia of a prolific family tree whose branches have spread through the South and West, and penetrated the North, at least as far as Philadelphia and New York.

At the date of the first patent this land was in Spotsylvania County, and has been, in succession, under the jurisdiction of Orange (1734), of Culpeper (1748 to 1792), and since the last date of Madison County.

Between the two streams is a beautiful eminence rising gradually from the banks of the Robinson river, which, in its rapid transit from the blue mountains in the distance, runs through valleys so thick with corn, that, in the language of the Psalmist, they laugh and sing, and then sweeps in a graceful curve around the hill, and receives into its bosom its meandering tributary. On the eminence stands a house, hoary with a century's mosses, and having in it a historical room originally dedicated to the

---

* So called in Fry and Jefferson's map and in Henning.

muses of music and the dance, in which William
Wirt, in his youth, played his pranks and wrote comedies; where Thomas Jefferson, in his journeys to
and from Washington, in his French Landau, re-
freshed himself with hospitable cheer, and which the
pioneer Methodist ministers made vocal with the
preached word, the voice of prayer and the songs of
Zion. This plantation now belongs to Jno. Lightfoot,
Esq., lineal descendant of the original patentee.

After a somewhat wide digression, I shall return
to this point of departure, and give illustrations of
the foregoing statements. It has been the uniform
tradition that Joshua Fry was born in Somersetshire,
England, and was educated at Oxford. But for the
uniformity of this tradition, I should be inclined to
doubt its truth. The name Fry is coeval with the
Colony. As early as 1623, as appears in a census of
that date, John Fry died in James City, and Henry
Fry at Flower de Hundred. In 1686 there was a
John Fry, of St. John's Parish, New Kent, who had
large landed interests in old Rappahannock County,
now Essex, the very county where our Joshua Fry
made his first appearance in Virginia. There are
several deeds now on record in Essex, by which this

NOTE.—This old mansion was 67 feet long, but only one story high. A second
story has been put upon it, and an addition of two stories erected in the rear.
A porch, the whole length of the house, has been added in front, and a smaller
one at the back. The "Historical Room," 24 x 19 feet, remains intact, except a new door opening on the front porch. The plantation, which originally
consisted of nearly 4,000 acres, is now divided into seven or eight farms. This
house was built by Henry Fry, (son of Col. Joshua Fry), when he came from
Albemarle to live in Culpeper, about 1766.

John Fry conveyed lands in Essex to divers parties. On the other hand, in the visitation of Somerset County, England, by Sir Thomas Phillips, privately printed, as I learn from Mr. Spofford, the accomplished Librarian of Congress, there is a pedigree of Fryes of Carrington, (1623) and later, in which the name is spelled with a final *e*. Gov. Dinwiddie's Commission to Col. Joshua Fry has the final *e* also. But in the records of Albemarle County, where Col. Joshua Fry signed his own name many times, the present form, Fry, is observed.

It is remarkable how many variations of the orthography of the same name occur in the records of a century. There are ten clergymen of the Church of England now in charge of parishes there, who spell their names Fry.

But, returning from this digression and accepting, as true, the tradition that Col. Joshua Fry was born in England, we have no means of determining the date of his migration to Virginia. We first made his acquaintance in the Parish Register, as Vestryman, and in the Records of the Court, as Commissioner (Magistrate) of Essex County, between 1710 and 1720. Here he married the widow of Col. Hill, a large landed proprietor on the Rappahannock river. Her maiden name was Mary Micou, and she was the daughter of Paul Micou, physician and surgeon, a Huguenot exile from persecution in France. Paul Micou, it is thought, brought his wife, and perhaps, some of his elder children with him. He certainly brought his library, pictures and plate. One of his daughters married John Lomax, the grand-father of the learned jurist and author, the late Judge John T. Lomax, sometime Professor of Law (U. Va.), Justice of the Court of Appeals, and so long one of the pillars of the Episcopal Church in Fredericksburg, Va. Another daughter married Moore Faunt Le Roy, a man of mark in his day, and the ancestor of the family of that name in Virginia.

I know of no other person in our history of like social position, wealth, capacity, character, and public services, as Col. Fry, about whom there is so little to be found in print, and that little so scattered in infinitesmal items. We have to trace his career by the posts of honor which he filled, as we would track the general of an army by the names of his battles, in ignorance of the details of his campaigns.

The next appearance of Col. Fry to public view is at Williamsburg, (1728–29). In the deed of the Surviving Trustees, who were Rev. Commissary Blair and Rev. Peter Fouace, transferring the property of William and Mary College to the Professors and Masters, they say : That, in pursuance of the trust confided to them, they had established two schools in Theology, and appointed as Professors thereof, the Rev. Bartholomew Yates and the Rev.

NOTE.—James Roy Micou, the present venerable Vestryman of his parish, and Clerk of Essex County, is of the fifth generation in descent from the ancestral Paul Micou, who left large estates to his children. His tombstone, on the Old Port Micou Estate, is, or was, before the war, extant, with the inscription : "Here lies the body of Paul Micou, who departed this life 22 May, 1736, in the 78th year of his age."

Francis Fontaine ; two schools in Philosophy, and appointed Rev. Mr. Dawson and Mr. Irvine, to those chairs. They established a Grammar School, and made Mr. Joshua Fry, of Williamsburg, master of it. He was afterwards advanced to the chair of Mathematics ; but of the duration of his connection with the College, or of the incidents which character-ized it, I have been only able to find these two items. In the extant records is the following entry :

"The foundation of the President's House was laid on the 30th of July, 1732. The President, (Rev. James Blair), Mr. Dawson, (who succeeded Blair as Commissary), Mr. Fry, Mr. Stith, (historian), and one Fox, laying the first five bricks in order, one after another."

In the Virginia Gazette, (the first newspaper in Virginia), the following article is found :

WILLIAMSBURG, Jan. 5th, 1738.

"Towards the close of the last session of Assem-bly, a proposition was presented to the House by Mr. Joshua Fry, Major Robert Brooke, and Major Wm. Mayo, to make an exact survey of the Colony, and print and publish a map thereof, in which shall be laid down the bays, navigable rivers, with the soundings, counties, parishes, towns, and gentlemen's seats, with whatever is useful or remarkable, if the House should see fit to encourage the same."

NOTE —The College, it will be remembered, with many of its records, have been repeatedly burned ; and during the late occupation by Federal troops, books and MSS. were carried off, and among them the old Vestry Book of Brewton Parish.

But as the said proposition was presented too late in the session, it was ordered that the consideration thereof should be postponed to the next session of Assembly. (Historical Register, vol. 4, p. 150, from Virginia Gazette).

It is not worth while to say what a precious treasure such a work would have been to after generations. This proposition is not alluded to in Henning, and the presumption is, that nothing came of it. It is chiefly interesting now in connection with the map executed some years after by Fry and Jefferson, showing that Fry had such a work in contemplation many years before he made his map.

One authority, (Drake) says that after the resignation of his professorship he was a member of the House of Burgesses, and of the King's Council. But whether he represented the College, or the County of Goochland, or Albemarle, is not known

CHAPTER II.

The next trace of Mr. Fry, is in the new County of Albemarle, which was cut off from Goochland by Act of Assembly, in September, 1744. Joshua Fry was living at that time on Hardware River, near Carter's Bridge, between Charlottsville and Scottsville.

The Act of Assembly establishing the County of Albemarle, provided, that, after the last day of

NOTE.—I am indebted to Mr. R. A. Brock, Secretary Virginia Historical Society, and F. R. Herson, for this reference.

December, ending, a Court should be organized. Accordingly, on the 28th of February, 1745, the Commissioners appointed for the new County, met, and the minute-book gives their names, viz.: Joshua Fry, Peter Jefferson, Allen Howard, Wm. Cabell, Joseph Thompson, and Thomas Bellew. A Commission of the Peace, directed to these persons, and a dedimus protestatum for administering the oath were openly read. Whereupon, Allen Howard and Wm. Cabell administered the oath prescribed by Act of Parliament to be taken, instead of oath of Allegience and Supremacy, and the Abjuration oath to Joshua Fry and Peter Jefferson, who took the same, and then subscribed to the Abjuration and the Test. Then Allen Howard and Wm. Cabell administered to Joshua Fry and Peter Jefferson the oath of Justice of the Peace, and the oath of Justice of the County Court in Chancery. On the same day the Court, composed of these Justices, met, Joshua Fry presided, and signed the minutes. He continued to be the presiding Justice of the Peace till August, 1748, probably much longer ; but the minute books of the Court from 1748 to 1775 are entirely lost.

At the first Court, Wm. Randolph produced his commission, and was sworn in as Sheriff ; Joshua Fry produced his commission, and qualified as Surveyor ; Edward Gray was sworn as King's Attorney.

It was ordered that Joshua Fry, gentleman, will meet the persons Goochland hath appointed, to run the dividing line between Goochland and Albemarle.

At the second court, Fry, Cabell, Jefferson and Bellew were present. Thomas Turpin was sworn in as Assistant Surveyor to Joshua Fry, March 28, 1745. A commission from the Honorable, the Lieutenant Governor, to Joshua Fry, Esq., to be County Lieutenant of Albemarle; Peter Jefferson to be Lieutenant Colonel; and Allen Howard, Major, was produced by Joshua Fry, and they were qualified.

The organization of a County Court affords an opportunity of paying a tribute in passing, to this "reflection of the old Shire system of England," which will not be impertinent to the purpose of this memoir. And this I find already done for me by Dr. Wm. Palmer, in his very able introduction to the Calendar of State Papers, which I take the liberty of abridging at the risk of marring the style. The County Lieut., its chief officer, originally called Commander of Plantations, was in England generally a knight, so in Virginia he was "a gentleman," and generally a large land-holder. He governed the County, and upon him rested the responsibility of a faithful execution of the laws. He could call out the militia when occasion demanded, and account to the Governor and Council for his conduct. The officers of the militia were subject to his orders, and he could even organize courts martial. He was as much a representative of the Governor and Council at Williamsburg as the latter were of the Council at London. The members of the County Court were men of substance and influence, and exponents of what was pure in character and patriotic in purpose. The records show many instances in which gentlemen refused to sit upon the bench with those who were habitual swearers or drunkards, or who were otherwise of such demeanor as was inconsistent with their sense of decorum.

To such a standard of virtue was legitimately traced the tone of public sentiment so long prevalent in the official administration of affairs in Virginia, when the Justice of the Peace was a true exemplar, and the people regarded the County Squire as the impersonation of virtue, dignity and decorum. For County Surveyors, intelligent and educated persons were required to submit to an examination by the learned Professors and Masters of William and Mary College.

It is worthy of note that a majority of the members of the Court in Albemarle, viz.: Col. Wm. Cabell, Peter Jefferson, Bellew and Thomas Turpin were assistant surveyors to Col. Fry. In June, 1746, Col. Fry reported and filed in court 150 tracts of land. In June, 1747, he returned 68 tracts, and in July 150 tracts, all in Albemarle, surveyed by him.

NOTE 1.—We commend to our readers Dr. Palmer's Introduction. It is not only valuable as an exposition of our historical documents, but it is a model of style. The picture of the County Clerk of olden time is a gem.

NOTE 2.—Peter Jefferson was the son of Thomas Jefferson, of Osborne, Chesterfield Co. He was born in 1708, and married Jane, daughter of Isham Randolph, of Dunginess. He had six daughters and two sons, of whom Thomas, Pres. U. S., was the elder. Thomas Turpin (descended from Philip Turpin, Yorkshire, Eng., who married Martha Skirm, of Hanover Co.) married an aunt of Thomas Jefferson, President.

I am indebted to Mr. Alexander Brown, of Union Hill, Nelson Co., a gentleman of antiquarian tastes and studies, for memoranda from the " Cabell Papers " of many entries of land in Albemarle, Amherst, Campbell, Buckingham, and Bedford, made by Col. Fry, from 1747 to 1753, inclusive. The entries in his own name (not withdrawn or transferred) amount to 9,000 acres. There are also entries made in the name of his son, Henry. Several of these tracts of land are mentioned in Col. Fry's Will. There are also entries with Thomas Turpin and Thomas Bellew, and one in Rev. Mr. Dawson's name, for 15,000 acres.

One object in giving the foregoing details of Col. Fry's work at home, is to give the reader some conception of his extraordinary industry and energy, as

NOTE 3.—There were three Wm. Cabells in succession : Dr. Wm. Cabell, the immigrant, born in Warminster, England, March 9, 1700, died in Virginia 1774. He was the friend and assistant surveyor to Col. Fry. He entered the first land west of Rockfish River 1735, extending thence along the Fluvanna (as James River above the mouth of the Rivanna was then called) 20 miles, thus extending the settlements 30 miles westward, when in the words of his orders in Council " no other man would attempt it." This land embraced about 8,000 acres of James River bottom. In 1741 he moved on it to keep off squatters, and there being nò field for his profession, he became assistant surveyor to Col. Wm. Mayo—after his death (1744) to Col. Fry till his death (1754). He then resumed the practice of his profession. From an entry in his diary (for which I am indebted to Mr. Alex. Brown, of Union Hill) we learn that Dr. Cabell " visited (1763) Madame Mary Fry " (she died, 1770), and in September, 1770, he says : " Attended Col. John Fry's wife with dead child three nights and two days." Col. Wm. Cabell, of Union Hill, was the son of the foregoing, and being a man of large landed possessions and wide business relations, and having filled many public offices, he had a large accumulation of valuable papers, including those of Rev. Robert Rose, a cousin of Patrick Henry, much of which have unhappily been destroyed. His, is one of the portraits, and Union Hill one of the scenes, in Mr. Grigsby's elegant historical picture of the Convention of 1776. Col. Wm. Cabell, Junior, was the son of Col. Wm., Sr., and the grandfather of the Hon Wm. Rives. This family, in each generation, were wardens and pillars of the Episcopal Church.

illustrated by the fact that, in the intervals between his engagements at home, he was discharging most honorable public trusts confided to him by the Governor. Thus in 1745 he was one of the Commissioners of the Crown for marking the line from the headsprings of the Rappahannock River to the headsprings of the Potomac, defining the western limit of the Northern Necks with his friend and co-laborer, Peter Jefferson. He was one of the Commissioners of the Crown in continuing the line between Virginia and North Carolina. In the same year, with the same colleague, he finished the map of Virginia, since known as Fry and Jefferson's Map. In 1752 he was one of the Commissioners for Virginia in negotiating the Treaty of Logstown.

These important and laborious trusts were discharged, it will be noted, in the intervals of the business done at home, as County Lieut., Presiding Justice, and Surveyor of Albemarle Co. Of these honorable achievements I proceed to give some details in their historical order, which will enable the general reader to appreciate them.

CHAPTER III.

AND FIRST OF NORTHERN NECK.

Those versed in the history of the State need hardly be reminded that the Lords Fairfax, by intermarriage with the heiress of Lord Culpeper, became the proprietors of that princely domain known as

the Northern Neck, and containing all the land between the Potomac and the Rappahannock rivers,
from their fountains to the Chesapeake Bay. As
soon as adventurous speculators began to enter lands
along these rivers towards the mountains, a contest
arose between the agents of the Crown and those of
Lord Fairfax, as to which of divers branches was the
main stream of the Potomac and of the Rappahannock, and where were their fountains. Upon the
question whether the Northern branch of the Rappahannock. or the Southern branch [called Rapid
Ann] was the Rappahannock proper, depended the
titles to all the land in the present counties of Culpeper, Madison, and Rappahannock.

In 1733, Lord Fairfax, proprietor of the Northern
Neck, petitioned the King in Council for a "Commission for running out and marking the limits of his
Patent." Accordingly, three Commissioners on the
part of the Crown, viz.: Col. Wm. Byrd, of Westover ; John Robinson, of Piscataway, and John
Grymes, of Brandon, Middlesex, were appointed.
Lord Fairfax, on his part, designated Wm. Beverly,
Wm. Fairfax, and Chas. Carter. They were author-
ized to summon witnesses, take depositions, and em-
ploy surveyors, chain-carriers, and markers. The
surveyors were Thomas and Mayo. They met in
Fredericksburg, September 26, 1736, began their
work on October 12, and finished it on December
14th. Col. Byrd has left a very humorous narrative
of their survey. Separate reports were made and re-

ferred to the Council for Plantation Affairs, which decided that the line ought to begin at the head-spring of the South Branch of the Rappahannock [the Rapid Ann,] and run northwest to the point where the Potomac River rises. This report was confirmed by the King in Council [April 11, 1745], and an order issued for the appointment of other Commissioners to run and mark the line,* agreeably

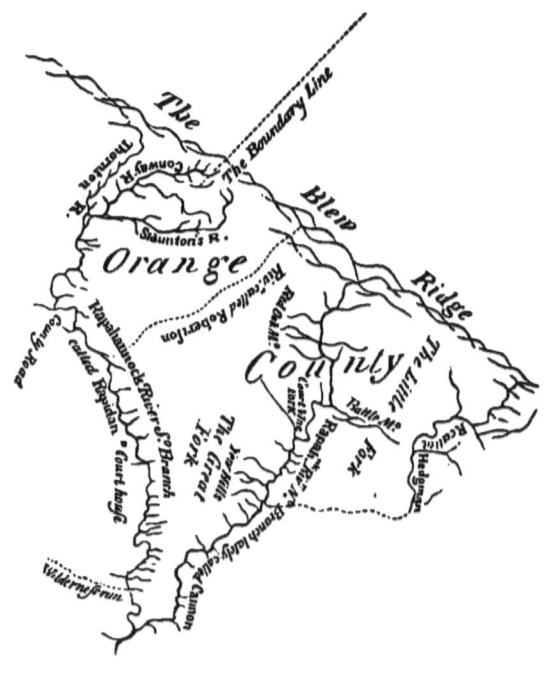

NOTE —The line marked may be seen in the accompanying section of their map. The journal of the Commissioners, with many other valuable documents referred to by Commissioner C. J. Faulkner, in his Report to Gov. Floyd (1832), were abstracted (stolen) from the State Library during the occupation of Richmond by the Federal troops. The reader is referred to the Byrd Papers and to the author's " History of St. Mark's Parish " for further details.

There is a copy of Hon. C. J. Faulkner's Report on Kercheval's " History of the Valley of Virginia."

to this decision. The new Commission consisted of the same persons on the part of Lord Fairfax, and on the part of the Crown Col. Joshua Fry, Col. Luns-ford, and Major Peter Hedgeman.

They began their survey on September 18, 1746, and on October 19 they planted the Fairfax Stone at the point which had been designated by the preceding Commissioners as the true headspring of the Potomac River.

A joint report [with neat maps and field notes by the surveyors Thomas and Major Wm. Mayo] were made to the authorities in England, and the controversy terminated.

CHAPTER IV.

THE BOUNDARY LINE BETWEEN VIRGINIA AND NORTH CAROLINA.

In 1749, Col. Fry and his friend, Peter Jefferson, were commissioned on the part of Virginia, to continue the boundary line between Virginia and North Carolina, which had been run, in 1728, from the sea to Peter's Creek, by Col. Wm. Byrd, Wm. Dandridge and Richard Fitzwilliams, with Thomas and Mayo as surveyors.

Fry and Jefferson continued the line from Peter's Creek (in the present County of Patrick, Va.) to Steep Rock Creek. This line was not completed to the Tennessee River till 1778, by Dr. Thomas

Walker and David Smith, on the part of Virginia.
They had great difficulty in finding the place where
Fry and Jefferson ended their line, on account of the
timber which had died in the mean time. It was
fixed by astronomical observations. (These Reports
may be seen in 9th H. 9, 562.)

CHAPTER V.

FRY AND JEFFERSON'S MAP.

A Collection of the Colonial Maps is an interesting and suggestive study. Capt. John Smith's map
is the first and the basis of all the others. It is
founded upon his personal observations, and upon
conjectures suggested by the Indians and others, and,
considering the circumstances in which his work was
done, it is remarkably well done. Mr. Jefferson says
that Fry and Jefferson's map, 1749, was the first
founded upon actual surveys. But there lies before
me a map drawn in 1760. Its title is, " Virginia and
Maryland, as planted and inhabited this present year,
1760; surveyed and exactly drawn by the only labour
and endeavour of Augustin Herman Bohemiensis." *

NOTE.—On this map are some curious observations. The land (he says)
between James and Roanoke Rivers is for the most part sunken and swampy,
and therein harbour Tigers, Bears and other devouring creatures. The heads
of York River (he says) issue out of marshy ground, and not out of mountains,
as other rivers. At the fountains of Chickahominy he places what he calls the
" Golden or Brass Hill, with the springs that issue from the hill is a glistening
sand like the filings of brass." I have also a map of the United States, with
the British Territories and those of Spain, according to the Treaty of 1784,
and Bowen's Map of the British and Spanish Dominions in North America,
according to the Definitive Treaty of Paris. The author is indebted to his
friend and relation, Wm. Green, LL.D., of Richmond, a gentleman whose
library is rich in historical treasures, and who is himself a " walking library,"
for kindly presenting him with these maps. Mr. Joseph Horner, the Antiquary of Warrenton, Va., has a copy of Henry's Map of Virginia. I have,
too, Mayo's Map of the Northern Neck, 1736.

The next in my collection is Fry and Jefferson's map, of which I have two editions.

One of these is on a reduced scale, including Maryland, parts of Pennsylvania and New Jersey, and "the most inhabited parts of Virginia."

It was made at the Photo-Lithographic Institute, Oxford St., London, 1775. The other is a French edition of the entire map of Virginia, and is entitled, "Carte de la Virginie et Maryland, dresse sur la grande carte de Messrs. Josué Fry et Pierre Jefferson, par Le Sr. Robert de Vaugondy, Geographe du Roi, 1755."

On this map the seat of Col. Joshua Fry, on Hardware River, in Albemarle County, is marked. The map in Jefferson's Notes of that part of Virginia east of the Alleghany Mountains, is taken from Fry and Jefferson's map. There lies before me, too, a copy of the Second Edition of Jno. Mitchell's Map of the British and French Dominions in North America, drawn originally in 1750.

CHAPTER VI.

THE TREATY OF LOGSTOWN.

The next trust committed to Col. Fry by the Governor was his appointment, in 1752, to be one of the Commissioners to negotiate the Treaty of Logstown, an Indian village on the right bank of the Ohio River, about eighteen miles below the present site of Pittsburg, which last was called Fort Du Quesne by the French and Fort Pitt by the English. A few words as to the incidents which led to this treaty, the parties to it, and the points settled by it, will not be impertinent. In 1749, the Ohio Company, composed of Mr. Hanbury and other leading merchants of London, and planters in Virginia, (among whom were Lawrence Washington and Thomas Lee, President of the Council,) was chartered by the British Government, which granted to them 600,000 acres of land in the valley of the Ohio River. Their objects being commercial as well as territorial, they took measures for exploring the country and establishing trading posts among the Indians. In 1750 they appointed Christopher Gist, an adventurous woodsman from the Yadkin, North Carolina, as their agent.

He explored the country for several hundred miles north of the Ohio, and as far south as the Falls. In 1751 he continued his explorations up the south side of the Ohio to the Kanawha River. His journal is still extant. The jealousy of the French was excited, and the Company's agents at their trading posts were seized and carried off. The policy both of the English and of the French was to gain the favor and co-operation of the Indians, who held the balance of power. The Ohio Company suggested to Virginia a treaty with the Indians at Logstown, and appointed Gist as their agent. The Government of Virginia adopted the suggestion, and appointed Col. Joshua Fry, Col. Lunsford Lomax and Col. James Patton as their Commissioners. The Shawnee

Mingo and Delaware Tribes were also represented. The Treaty was concluded on June 13th, 1752. By the Treaty the Indians bound themselves not to molest any settlement on the southeast side of the Ohio. They also became allies of the English, and rendered valuable service in the ensuing year. Gist was one of the first settlers in the valley of the Monongahela, and induced other families to keep him company. (See Marshall's Washington, v. 1, p. 25 ; Spark's, 2, p. 27 ; Irving's Washington.)

In the instructions to the Commissioners it is said, that " as doubts had arisen about the construction of the Treaty of Lancaster, and as it had been alleged that the " Six Nations " thought themselves imposed upon, it was necessary to have the subject explained.

It is the same old story of which we have had so many rehearsals since. For the chiefs, in acknowledging that the Lancaster deed was " for a quantity of land in Virginia which you and the whites have a right to," say (mournfully) but we " never understood, until you told us yesterday, that the lands then sold were to extend farther towards the setting sun than the hill on the other side of the Alleghany hills.

On the French edition of Fry's map is this inscription : " Route Indienne par La Traite de Lancastre." It is a marked line in the valley of Virginia on the headwaters of the North Shenandoah River.

NOTE.—In addition to the authorities just cited, I acknowledge my obligations to Lyman C. Draper, LL.D., the accomplished and courteous Secretary of the Wisconsin Historical Society, who has a very rare, if not unique volume upon this subject.

After his return from Logstown, Col. Fry met
with a severe accident, as appears from the following
entry in the diary of Dr. Wm. Cabell, (before quoted)
viz., Oct. 16, 1752. " Left the Doctor's in company
with Col. Fry, who had a fall from his horse near
Deep Run Chapel, and by it broke his collar bone
and bruised' his ribs, if not broke them. Taken in
and kindly treated by Samuel Allen."

CHAPTER VII.

COL. FRY APPOINTED TO COMMAND THE VIRGINIA FORCES. — HIS COMMIS- SION. — HIS DEATH, BURIAL, AND EPITAPH.

England and France had been watching each
other with eagle eyes on the Ohio and its tributaries.
The little war-cloud which had been hovering in the
northwestern horizon, now put on a darker and more
angry aspect, with occasional flashes, portentous of a
coming storm. The youthful Washington, in his
twenty-first year, had been sent by the Governor of
Virginia on a mission of peace to the Commander of
the French, which failed of its end. The great contest for supremacy in the valley of the Mississippi, so
big with momentous issues to the material interests
of England, America and France, and to the cause of
constitutional government, civilization and religion,
was about to begin in earnest. The Ohio Company,
composed chiefly of merchants in London and plan-

ters in Virginia, and having a grant of 600,000 acres of land in the Ohio valley, was active in stimulating resistance to French aggression. The bugle sounded to battle. The General Assembly of Virginia appropriated £10,000 to swell the Virginia Regiment, as it was called. Governor Dinwiddie, in looking for a proper person to command the Virginia forces, fixed his eye on Col. Joshua Fry, and gave him the chief command.

The following is a copy of the commission from the original now in the possession of his great-great-grandson, Mr. Wm. O. Fry, of Charlottesville, Virginia.

TO JOSHUA FRY.

"His Majesty, by his royal instructions, commanded me to send a proper number of forces, to erect and maintain a fort at the Monongahela and Ohio Rivers; and, having a good opinion of your loyalty, conduct and ability, I do hereby institute, appoint and commission you to be Colonel and Commander-in-Chief of the forces now raising, to be called the Virginia Regiment, with which and the artillery, arms and ammunition, necessary provisions and stores, you are with all possible dispatch to proceed to the said Fort of Monongahela, and there act according to your instructions." Washington was the Lieutenant-Colonel of this regiment, and went in advance to clear a road for the artillery which was to follow with Col. Fry, from Alexandria. Washington left Alexandria, April 27, 1754. The artillery was to be conveyed up the Potomac to Will's Creek. Having reached the mouth of Will's Creek (Fort Cumberland) on the Potomac River, Col. Fry was suddenly arrested by the hand of death, 31st of May, 1754. Had he lived, who can tell what he might have achieved by his engineering skill, and by his experience of life in the wilderness, and his personal knowledge of the country which he had before traversed. Washington succeeded to the command, and, in due time, had the " all cloudless glory to free his country." And his name and fame are now co-incident with civilization, and promise to be co-eval with Time.

In a cotemporary notice of Col. Fry's death, it was said : " He was a man of so clear a mind, so mild a temper, and so good a heart that he never failed to enjoy the love and esteem of all who knew or were connected with him, and he was universally lamented."

I have never seen in print the circumstances of Col. Fry's burial, but I find in the family papers a manuscript which is not accredited to any authority, giving the following brief notice, which is beautiful in its incidents, and will be a fitting peroration to the brief memoir of a man whose memory has nearly lapsed from the minds of the present generation, but which should not be suffered to perish, and which, I would fain hope, my humble tribute may, in some measure, serve to revive and to hand down to the generation to come.

"Col. Fry was buried near Fort Cumberland, near Will's Creek, on May 31, 1754."

Washington and the army attended the funeral ; and on a large oak tree, which now stands as a tomb and a monument to his memory, Washington cut the following inscription, which can be read to this day : " Under this oak lies the body of THE GOOD, THE JUST AND THE NOBLE FRY."

Col. Fry left five children, viz :

1.   JOHN, born May 7, 1737.
2.   HENRY, born October 19, 1738.
3.   MARTHA, born May 18, 1740. -
4.   WILLIAM, born Feb. 6, 1743, died July 1, 1760.
5.   MARGARET, born May 15, 1744.

Mrs. Margaret Fry, wife of Col. Joshua Fry, died August 20, 1772.

CHAPTER VIII.

COL. FRY'S LAST WILL.

Col. Fry's will was admitted to record in the County Court of Albemarle, Va., August 8, 1754. His wife, and his friend, Peter Jefferson, qualifying as executors.

NOTE.—Fry Washington found among Col. Fry's papers, a blank commission of Cap'ain, which he gave to Adam Stephen, afterwards Gen'l Adam Stephen.

His will begins thus :

In the name of God, Amen.

I, Joshua Fry, of the County of Albemarle, being in good health and of sound memory, do make and declare this to be my last will and testament. He gives to his dear wife, Mary, the land on which he lives, and also that part of his land in Culpeper, which lies between the Robinson River and Crooked Run, including the old quarter, during her life. He also gives her one-third part of his slaves for life, and all his household goods. He gives all his slaves to be divided among his children, when his son Henry becomes of age. The profits arising from his lands and slaves, (excepting those devised his wife for life), he allots to the maintenance and education of his children, to the saving of his lands. He gives to his son John, and his heirs, the land on which the testator now lives, after the death of his mother ; he also gives his son John, his Eppes tract and the one adjoining it, also 400 acres on Tye River, and his part of the order in council, to him and Twipin, adjoining ; also, 4 other tracts of 900 acres. He gives to his son Henry, all his lands in Culpeper, on the Robinson River and its branches, his mother retaining that part between the Robinson River and C. Run, during her life. My son Henry, he says, has a tract in his own name on Bolling's Creek of Fluvanna, the patent for which is three years old. Peyton Randolph is to attend to its continuance, but if it lapses and a fresh grant be taken by me, I give it to my son Henry, and if the entry is in the name of my son John, I command him to make a title to his brother Henry, on pains of forfeiting to his said brother, the lands on Briery Creek, which in that event, I give to my son Henry. He gives to his son William his lands on Willis' branches, and on Glover's road, containing 1100 acres, he having in his own name, two tracts on Tongue quarter, and Buck and Doe Creeks.

He gives to his daughter, Martha, his *mine* tract on the Meadows, and another adjoining, and another tract on the Milestone branch, adjoining Harvies Green Spring Tract.

He gives to his daughter, Margaret, his land on Porridge Creek, containing 2018 acres, my daughters having in their own names, two tracts on Rocky Run, to which I have added 400 acres on both sides of Buffalo River, which they must divide equally between them.

He gives to his friend Col. Jefferson, all his surveying instruments.

He gives the residue of his estate, including the money arising from the sale of his lands in Brunswick, which he empowers his executors to sell, to be equally divided between his wife and children. Finally, he appoints his dear wife and his friend, Col. Peter Jefferson, and his son John, executors of his will. .

Witnesses, } JOHN MARTIN, SAMUEL COBBS.

Col. Fry, when he lay down to die at the mouth of Wills Creek, (then a howling wilderness), little dreamed that in a few years his youthful Lieutenant, Washington, would be the Commander-in-Chief of a Continental Army and the chief instrument of plucking from the British crown (to which they were both then loyal and loving subjects), its brightest jewel, and would be the first President of a great American Republic, recognized and revered by all its citizens, as the Father of his country. As little did he dream that the son (of his other Lieutenant, Peter Jefferson), then a school-boy, after a brief interval, should succeed Washington in the same office, or their common county of Albemarle, should found a University which should overshadow and eclipse his own beloved William and Mary. It did not enter into his imagination that his assistant (Surveyor), Dr. William Cabell, would be the progenitor of a race that should illustrate the history of Virginia, in the halls of legislation, and the academies of learning, and represent the American Republic at the Court of France, to drive whose subjects from the soil of Virginia, he had girded on his armour and was about to lay down his life.

Much less did he dream that before the celebration of its first Centennial, the great American Republic should be convulsed and rent by civil war, and that his own descendants would be found fighting under hostile banners on both sides of the bloody chasm. It is a merciful Providence which hides the future of time and sense from our eyes. Could we foresee the developments of the next half century, they might make each particular hair stand on end.

We might see   *   *   Rampant war
"Yoke the red dragons of her iron car
And Peace and Mercy banished from the plain,
Spring on the viewless winds to Heaven again."

Or we might see the goddess of reason so-called), enthroned in the Capitol, after the fashion of the French, or the Commons dispersed at the point of the bayonet, after the example of Cromwell; or an Emperor in the seat of Washington, and the empire sold at auction after the manner of the Romans.

But thank God this world is not the last scene in the drama of Providence. The eye of faith passes the bounds of time and sense, and reveals another scene, where all wrongs will be righted, where might will not be the master, but the hand-maid of right— all dark Providences be illuminated—truth triumphant—the only law be love—into which all the attributes of God and all the ways of His Providence shall be seen to meet and melt, as all the colors of the rainbow meet and blend into a ray of pure perfect light.

"God is Light and God is Love."

Without such a God, history would be unintelligible—an inexplicable enigma to thought and a crushing weight upon the heart.

PREFACE TO GENEALOGY.

The candid reader will please mark, learn and inwardly digest this preface, before he plunges into the pedigree.

Genealogies seem to be the outgrowth of an instinct common to the human family, which raises a strong presumption, that this instinct was implanted for wiser ends, than the ministering to personal vanity or family pride.

The oldest histories (we are told by high authority are drawn upon a genealogical basis). " The Pedigrees preserved in the book of Genesis are the scaffolding to the temple of universal history, and the Bible regarded as a whole, is a genealogical collection of surpassing interest and value."

But as these, (it may be said), were designed to subserve special religious ends, it will be pertinent to remind the reader, that the earliest Greek histories are Genealogies, and the " Gens and Familæ familas of the Romans," "the clans of the Celts and the common patronymics of the Saxons" are examples of this instinct, and of its historical uses.

The errors and discrepancies which have crept into the chronicles of the Jews, notwithstanding the religious care with which they have been preserved, show how difficult it is to keep them out of such records. Volumes have been written by scholars to reconcile the discrepancies in the books of Chronicles and Ezra, and in the Genealogies of our blessed Saviour himself, and still they are subjects of dispute.

An author cannot spin Genealogies out of his own brain, as the goddess sprung complete from the brain of Jupiter. He can only collate and digest materials gathered from various and often conflicting authorities. They then pass into the hands of copyists, and are thence committed to the tender mercies of that most formidable of all steam engines, the press. It will be a marvel if a family can make all these perilous passages without the loss of some member or suffering such dislocations and fractures that they often can hardly be recognized. If therefore, one does not find himself married to his grandmother, he ought to be happy, instead of regarding himself as the victim of malice aforethought or culpable carelessness.

The worst crimes that can be charged upon Authors and Printers when they maim or kill people before their time is what the lawyers call "involuntary manslaughter." The present writer used to think the Litany of the Church perfect. But since he has been so rash as to perpetrate pedigrees, he is inclined to believe that the litany would be improved by one more petition,

From writing Genealogies—
Deliver us.

THE GENEALOGY.

The readers special attention is called to the following abbreviations, viz.: *b* for born,—*d* for died,—*m* for married,—*s* for son,—*dau.* for daughter,—*ch* for child,—*d. s. p.*—died without issue.

Col. Joshua Fry *m* Mrs. Hill, whose maiden name was Mary Micou, *dau.* of Paul Micou, (Physician and Surgeon), who was an exile from France, to Essex County, Virginia. Their issue was:

I. Col. John Fry, Vestryman of St. Ann's Parish, Albemarle, Va., *b* May 7, 1737. He *m* Miss Adams, and had issue, Joshua, William and Tabitha.

Issue of Joshua [2] Fry, Vestryman of St. Ann's Parish, and Peachy Walker, his wife, who was the *dau.* of Dr. Thomas Walker of Castle Hill, Albemarle, Va. They moved to Kentucky. He was a renowned classical teacher in Va. and in Ky.

Issue 1. Dr. John [2] Fry *m* Judith Harrison, still surviving, in her 90th year, and walks to church every Sunday; their issue is:

1. Peachy, *m* Mr. Montgomery; 2, John; 3, Cary H. General U. S. A., commended by General Taylor for gallantry at Buena Vista; he is buried in Soldiers' Cemetery, San Francisco.

II. Thos. Walker, *s* of Joshua [2] Fry, *m* Betsy Smith and had issue, Gen'l. Speed Smith Fry, distinguished officer U. S. A., and other sons unknown to the Author; a *dau. m* Dr. Lewis Warner Green, President Hampden Sidney College, Va., and of Centre

College, Ky., other *daus.* were Mrs. Cox, Mrs. Barbee and Mrs. Winston.

William Fry, *s* of Col. John and grand-*s* of Col. Joshua [1] Fry, moved to Kentucky, *d* unmarried; of Tabitha, his sister, nothing is known except that she *m* in Kentucky, Boleo Cooke.

Issue of Martha, 2d *d* of Joshua [2] Fry, and David Bell, (Irish Merchant, Ky.) :

1. Joshua Fry Bell, (Danville) M. C. and distinguished orator.
2. Mrs. Beatty, wife of the President of Centre College, Ky.

Issue of 3d *dau.* of Joshua Fry and Judge John Green, Danville, Ky.:

1. Dr. Willis Green, (Frankfort), *m dau.* of Rt. Rev. B. B. Smith, Presiding Bishop of P. E. Church.
2. Peachy, *m* Rev. R. A. Johnstone, (Presbyterian) Danville, Ky.
3. Sarah, *m* married Jno. Borsley.
4. Rev. Joshua Fry Green, *d* 1854.
5. Susan, *m* James Weir, Boonsboro, Ky.
6. Rev. Wm. L. Green, Peoria, Illinois.

Judge Jno. Green *m* 2d, a *g-dau.* of Col. Thos. Marshall, and Thos. Marshall Green, Maysville, is their son.

NOTE.—Dr. Lewis W. Green was the youngest son of Willis Green, who was the son of Duff Green and Anne, daughter of Col. Henry Willis, by his third wife, Mrs. Mildred Gregory. She (Ann), was buried at Danville, Ky, and her tomb-stone still stands. Duff Green was the son of Robert Green, one of the first Vestrymen of St. Mark's Parish, Culpeper County, Va. 1730.

Issue of Mildred Ann, *dau.* of Joshua [2] Fry and Wm. C. Bullitt.[*]

1. Joshua Fry Bullitt, sometime Chief-Justice of Ky., and now of the Louisville Bar, who *m* Elizabeth R. Smith, and had issue: Joshua Fry, Jno. C. and James Bell Bullitt.

2. Alex. Scott Bullitt, *d* 1840.

3. John C. Bullitt, a leading member of Philadelphia (Pa.) Bar, (Author of a Review of Binney, on Habeas Corpus, and of a very able defence of Gen'l. Fitz John Porter, &c.) He *m* Therese Langhorn, and had issue: 1. Therese, *m* Dr. Coles, U. S. Navy.; 2. Wm. Christian, (Lawyer); 3, Julia.; 4, Logan McKnight.; 5, James Fry.; 6, Helen Key.; 7, Jno. C. Bullitt,

4. Martha Bell, *dau.* of Wm. C. Bullitt, *d* 1847.

5. Susan Peachy, *dau.* of Wm. C. Bullitt, *m* Archibald Dixon, Lieutenant-Governor of Ky., and U. S. Senator, and had issue: 1, Kate, *m* David Burbank.; 2. Wm. B.; 3, Thomas B.

6. Sarah Bell, *d* infant.

7. Helen Martin, *m* Dr. Henry Chenowith, and had issue: 1, Martha Ann, *m* John Stiles, (Louisville Bar); 2, Fanny Bell; 3, Susan B.; 4, Henry; 5, James.

8. Capt. Thomas Walker Bullitt, C. S. A., prominent lawyer, (Louisville), *m* Annie, *dau.* of

---

NOTE.—Wm. C. Bullitt, was the son of Alex. Scott Bullitt, 1st Lieutenant Governor of Kentucky, President of Convention, Ky, 1799, who married Priscella, daughter of Col. Wm. Christian, and Anne, sister of Patrick Henry, Va.

Chancellor Logan and Agatha, *g-g-dau.* of Col. Thomas Marshall. Issue: 1, Wm. Marshall; 2, James Bell; 3, Agatha Marshall; 4, Alex. Scott; 5, Mildred Ann.

9. James Bell Bullitt, C. S. A.. killed while carrying a Flag of Truce.

10. Henry Massie Bullitt. C. S. A., *m* Mary L. Frederick. He lives at Oxmoore, near Louisville, where his father was born and lived; his grand-father lived and died, and his great-grand-father Col. William Christian, (who was killed by the Indians), lived and was buried.

Issue of Lucy Gilmer, oldest *dau.* of Joshua ² Fry, and Judge Speed :

III.—Lucy Gilmer Fry, *m* Judge Jno. Speed, (his 2d wife), she *d* 1874, issue :

1. Lucy, *m* James Breckenridge, no issue.

2. James, Att-General, in Lincoln's Cabinet, now a lawyer of Louisville, who *m* Jane Cochrane and had issue : John Breckenridge, Henry, Charles, James, and Joshua.

3. Peachy, *dau.* of Judge Speed, *m* Austin Peay. issue : George Speed, and Eliza, who *m* Mr. Ward of the Louisville Bar.

4. Joshua Fry Speed, a wealthy citizen of Louisville, *m* Fanny Henning, no issue.

5. Wm. Speed, *m* 1st, Miss Philips ; *m* 2d, Miss Shallcross, who left one child, J. Breckenridge Speed.

6. Philip Speed, *m* Emma Keats, (niece of the Poet), issue :

1. Mary, *m* Mr. Tuley, Asst. Post-Master, Louisville.
2. George Keats, who *m* ———— and has seven children.
3. Lina, *m* Capt. Rogers, U. S. N. of Philadelphia.
4. Ella, *m* Thos. Crutcher, and left six children.
5 John Keats, connected with the *New York World* newspaper.
6. Alice *m* Harry, *s* of Col. Angus McDonald, Va.
7. Fanny.   8, Florence.

7. Smith, *s* of Judge Speed, *m* 1st, Miss Henning : *m* 2d, Miss Philips, issue several sons and daughters, names unknown to the author, except Mrs. J. Menifee.

8. Susan Fry, *dau.* of Judge Speed, *m* Benj. Davis, issue :

1. Lucy, *m* J. E. Hardy, and has a large family,
2. Eliza.
3. John Speed, who left one child.
4. Joshua.
5. Kate, *m* Dexter Hewitt, issue : 3 children.
6. Edward, Lieut. U. S. A.
7. Mary.
8. L. Rodgers, *m* Dr. Douglas Morton of Louisville, and had two children.
9. Martha, *dau.* of Judge Speed, *m* Mr. Adams, issue : Gilmer and Jesse.
11. Henry Fry, 2d *s* of Col. Joshua Fry and Mrs.

Hill, (Micou), was *b* October 19, 1738, *m*
(June 16, 1764), Sukey, *dau.* of Dr. Thomas
Walker, of Albemarle, (in her 17th year.)

Issue: 1. Margaret, *b* May 29, 1765, *m* Philip Lightfoot, and moved to Ky., issue unknown

11. Reuben, (*s* of Rev. Henry), *b* July 9, 1766, *d*
May 29, 1805), *m* October 16, 1788, Anne
Coleman, *dau.* Col. James Slaughter, of
Culpeper, Va., and sister of Capt. Philip
Slaughter, both officers of the old revolu-
tion. Issue :

1. Susan Peachy, *m* Matthew, *s* of Rev. Matthew
Maury, issue : six sons and two daughters,
their third *dau. m* Rev. F. B. Nash, (Epis-
copal), and left 8 children, one of whom
Rev. F. B. Nash, is an Episcopal Minister
at Ottawa, Ill. Reuben went to Oregon,
John to Louisville, and the others to
Owingsville, Ky.

11. Matilda, *dau.* of Reuben Fry and Ann Coleman Slaughter, *m* July 3, 1810, Francis
Fontaine, *s* of Rev. Matthew Maury of Albemarle, Va. and moved to Ky. 1818, (they
were both *g*-children of Dr. Thos. Walker.

Issue: 1. Reuben Thornton, M. D., *d* in Alabama,
leaving one *dau.* Eliza Thornton, who *m*
Mr. Winter, of Miss.

2. Rev. Matthew Fontaine, (Episcopal), Danville,
Ky., who *m* Miss Chipman of Vermont, and
had four children :

1. Francis Fontaine, M. D., Prof. in Philadelphia, who *m* Kate, *dau.* of Charles Ingersoll.
2. Austin C.; 3, James Robb.; 4, Eliza, who *m* Matthew Fontaine Maury, of Charlottsville, Va.
3. Sarah Slaughter, only *dau.* of Francis Fontaine Maury and Matilda Fry, *m* Rev. Edward Berkely, D. D., who was for 19 years Rector of Christ Church, Lexington, Ky., (where he baptised Hon. Henry Clay, in 1847, and buried him in 1852, and is now Rector of St. Peter's, St. Louis, Mo.

Issue : 1. Francis Maury, *m* P. H. Patriarch.
2. Mary Fairfax, *m* Wm. Ward Childs.
3. Matilda Fontaine, *m* Lorraine F., *s* of Rev. Alex. Jones, D. D., formerly of Richmond, Va.
4. Edward Fairfax, *m* Miss Hendee, of Georgia.
5. Sarah Thornton; 6, Charlotte; 7, James Henry Fry.

III.—Anne Clayton, *dau.* of Reuben Fry and Ann Coleman Slaughter, *m* (1820), Wm. Hope of Owingsville, Ky. Issue, 1, Ann M. *m* Col. R. T. Harvey, Huntington, W. Va., and had issue, 1, Thos. Hope, lawyer, who *m* Emma McCullough. 2, Fanny, a Nun of St. Joseph's Convent, Wheeling. 3, Clayton H., 4, Robt. Smith, M. D. of Wheeling, W. Va. 5, Wm. Hope, lawyer, Gallipolis, Ohio, *m* Anna Halliday and had

2. Thomas, *s* of Wm. Hope, *m* Mary Payne, and *d* in San Francisco, 1854.

3. Matilda, *dau.* of Wm. Hope, *m* Chapman Maupin and has issue : Fanny Clayton, who *m* Mr. Crawford, and has 3 children ; 2, Thos. H. *m* Miss Smith.; 3, Albert ; 4. Walker, all in Mo. Lucy *m* J. T. Doyle. Alice *m* Sampson.

Anne Clayton, *dau.* of Reuben Fry. *m* 2d, James Nounnan, issue : 1, Major James H. Nounnan, C. S. A., wounded four times, *m* Miss Harmer, has 2 children, lives in Utah.; 2d, Jos. Fry Nounnan, *m* Miss Fox, issue : Joseph, Nannie and Charles ; San Francisco.

IV.—Mary, *dau.* of Reuben Fry and Ann Clayton Slaughter, *m* Robert Nelson Smith, *g-s* of Gov. Page, Va. Vestryman and devout member of Episcopal Church for 40 years in Kentucky, and Lexington, Mo., where they both died, he in his 84th year. Issue : Eliza W. *m* Adjt.-Gen'l. McLane of Gen. Price's Staff C. S. A. Issue : 2, Nelson Smith ; 3, Hugh, *s* of R. N. Smith ; 4, Richard, died just after his election to Congress, in Santa Fee ; 5, Robert, M. D., *m* Miss Ruffner and had nine children. The only survivors of 12 children are Joseph, near Lexington, Mo. and Coleman, lawyer, Bates Co. Mo., *m* Miss Taylor.

V.—Joseph, *s* of R. Fry and A. C. Slaughter, (State Senator, eminent jurist, and Judge at Charleston and Wheeling, W.Va., *m* Miss Wilson of Charleston, issue: 1, James W. dec'd. 2, Jane A. *m* Judge Paul of Supreme Court, W. Va., and had issue, three children: Judge Fry, *m* 2d Elizabeth, *dau.* Rev. Dr. McElhenny, Louisburg, W. Va., issue : 1, Lucy Clayton, *m* Hon. H. M. Mathews, Governor, W. Va., and had issue : Lucile, Josephine and Wm. Gordon.

2, John Joseph, *s* of Judge Fry, killed at Manassa, July 21, 1861, C. S. A.

3, Henry, *m* L. B. Hoffnagle, and had issue : Frank, Lucy, Clayton, Lily, Josephine L. Elizabeth Ann.

4, Rebecca, *dau.* of Judge Fry, *m* Col. George M. Edgar, and had issue : Gertrude, Bessie Randolph, George and John Fry, Lily and Rose, twins.

5, William Wirt.

VI.—James Henry, *s* of Reuben Fry and A. C. Slaughter, Sheriff of Kanawha and State Senator, *m* two Misses Donally, and had issue :

1, Philip, 2, Mrs. Alvin Goshorn, who had 2 children.

3, Mary, *m* Lewis Wilson ; 4, Henry, 5, Joseph, 6, Sally.

VII.—Philip Slaughter, *s* of Reuben Fry and A. C. Slaughter, Clerk of Orange Co., Va. *m* Miss Anderson of Richmond, and had issue: Philip Henry, present Clerk of Orange, (*b* 1834), *m* Miss Oden, Martinsburg, W. Va., no issue.

2, Edmund M. killed at Manassas, September, 1862.

3, Thos. Slaughter, cotton factor in Mobile, *b* February 23, 1838, *m* December 6, 1865 Mary, *dau.* of Reuben Shorter of Columbus, Ga., and has issue : Charles Philip, Edmund Maury, Kate, Fanny Gordon and Mildred.

4. Charles Wm., Hot Springs, Arkansas, (*b* 1842), *m* Fanny Davis of Alabama and has two children.

5. Luther Conway, (*b* November 17, 1844,) Bank officer, Mobile.

6. Reuben Macon, Chicot Co., Arkansas, *m* Miss Hutchins, Natchez, and has three children. 7, Alexa. Maury, *d* infant.

III.—Martha, (*dau.* of Rev. Henry), *b* December 21, 1769, *d* October 17, 1828, *m* Goodrich Lightfoot, of Madison, Va. Issue :

1. Elizabeth, *m* Joseph Hume and had two children.

2. Susan, *m* Matthew Maury of Albemarle, issue, 7.

3. Maria, *m* Mr. Spence, of Wythe Co., no issue.

4. Catherine, *m* Jno. Mayer of Botetourt, issue, 5.

5. Margaret, *m* Dr. T. Patterson of Fincastle, no issue.

6. William, *m* Catherine Maury of Albemarle, issue, 10.

7. Wesley, *m* Miss Franklin of Amherst, issue, 4.

8. Frank, *m* Miss Fielder of Culpeper, issue :

    1. Col. Edward Lightfoot, C. S. A., now of Bethel Academy, Fauquier Co., who *m* Miss Chapin, and has issue.

    2. Fanny, *m* Col. Charles Crittenden, C. S. A. issue, 2 children.

    3. Mary, *m* Dr. James Herndon, who *d* a martyr nursing yellow fever at Fernandina. No issue.

9. Walker Lightfoot, Clerk of Culpeper Co., *d* single.

10. Edward, *m* Miss. Conner, and has issue :

    1. Virginia.

    2. John, *b* 1836, *m* 1st, *dau.* of Lewis Turner of Culpeper, and has issue, John and Lizzie, *m* 2d, Miss Hudgins of Richmond. Edward *m* 2d, Miss Ann Yancey, and is the only survivor of the children of Goodrich Lightfoot and Martha Fry.

IV.—Joshua, *s* of Rev. Henry, *b* May 17, 1769, *d* October 17, 1838, *m* November 24, 1793, Kitty Walker, (*b* July 1, 1772, *d* 1814.)

Issue : 1. Henry Belville, (*b* December 22, 1794, *d* February 14, 1836,) *m* Annie Clarke, issue :

1. Chas. Meriwether, Pres. Bank New York, who *m* Lizzie, *dau.* of B. Watkins Leigh, U. S. Senator, Jurist and Statesman of the first magnitude.

2. Kitty W. *m* W. D. Fry, of Madison.

3. Maria E. *m* Thos. Sparks. Issue, Anna, Marion, Clarke, Alice, Henry, Clara, John, Thomas (C. Meriwether.) Henry Belville *m* 2d, Lucy Clark. Issue :

1. Sarah A. *m* R. S. Thomas, Clerk of Madison Co., and has issue, Clara H., Henry W., Lucy, James, Mary, Sidney, Chas. Meriwether.

2. Mary E. *m* Jerry Garnett : issue, Belville, Milton, Lucy, Cabel, Selden, Willie H.

3. Clara H. *m* 12th September, 1877, Absalom G. Garnett.

11. Hugh Walker, (*s* of Joshua,) *b* January 22, 1796, *d* February 13, 1872, *m* 26th December, 1820, Maria White, *b* July 1, 1801. Issue : 1, Wm. Henry, *b* October 8, 1821, *m* May 8, 1844, Jane M. Watson, *b* Aug. 29,

1825. Issue 1, Hugh Walker, *b* Nov 14, 1846. 2, Anna Maria, *b* December 6, 1848. 3, Richard Watson, *b* November 3, 1850. 4, Wm. Henry, *b* August 15, 1852. Jane M., *b* May 23, 1854. 5, Peter Meriwether, *b* May 24, 1856. 6, Chas. Nelson, *b* April 31, 1858. 7, E. Shepherd, *b* December 27, 1859. 8, Edward Scott, *b* September 19, 1861, 9, Douglas Bland, *b* July 24, 1863. 10, M. Douglas, *b* September 22, 1867. 11, Susan Harris, *b* October 16, 1869.

John James, *s* of Hugh Walker, *b* February 5, 1824, *m* Mary Lewis of Albemarle, *b* Oct. 6, 1831. Issue :

1. Howell Lewis, *b* October 1, 1850. 2, Margaret Douglas, *b* July 12, 1852. 3, John Walker, *b* July 12, 1854. 4, Samuel Gordon, *b* October 13, 1856. 5, Infant. 6, Susan S. *b* October 13, 1859. 7, S. Standford, *b* January 3, 1863.

Hugh Walker, *s* of Hugh Walker, *b* April 14, 1826, *d* October 22, 1872, *m* Mary L. Davidson of Georgetown, D. C. Issue, Henry D. Fry, M. D., Washington City ; Mary Emily, *b* June 12, 1832, *m* 1st, Samuel Mitchell. Issue : Sam'l. P. *m* 2d, Nathaniel Shepherd, Richmond.

III.—Joshua Jefferson (*s* of Joshua,) *b* October 6, 1799. *m* May 4, 18?3. Sally Scott, *d. s p*

IV.—Mary, *b* January 29, 1801, *m* George Miller, issue, John, Mary, Lizzie, Joshua,

V,—S. Emily, *b* April 29, 1803, *m* Larkin Willis. Issue : Rev. E. J. Willis.

VI. Edward H., *b* September 2, 1804.

V.—Thomas Walker, (*s* of Rev. Henry,) *b* Oct. 24, 1770, *m* the widow of Clayton Slaughter, brother of Capt. Philip Slaughter—her maiden-name was Bourn. Thos. Walker, *m* 2d *dau.* Col. Abram Maury of Madison Co. Issue : Wm. Wirt and two others.

VI.—Henry, (*s* of Rev. Henry,) *m* Mildred, *dau.* of Rev. Mathew Maury, Rector of Fredericksville Parish, Albemarle, and had issue : 1, Mathew, *d. s. p.* 2, J. Frank, Commissioner of the Revenue in Albemarle, so well known and so much respected, who *m* Jan. 4, 1822. Mary I. *dau.* of Nelson Barksdale, and had issue : 1, T. Wesley, *b* June 23, 1823, *m* Sarah McLauren. Issue, 3 : 1, Edwin J. Fry, a leading banker of Marshall, Texas, who *m* Miss L. Rankin, and had two children. 2, Clara, who *m* I. F. Star, prominent at the Bar. 2, Mathew Henry (*s* of Jas. Frank,) *b* August 28, 1824, *m* Sarah, *dau.* of Alex. St. C. Heiskell, no issue. 3, Mildred J. (*dau.* of J. Frank,) *b* November 29, 1825, *m* James S. Barksdale of Albemarle. Issue : Mary Elizabeth, Francis

Nelson, Mildred Fry, Betty C. Lucy Maury.
4. Jno. Nelson, (s of J. Frank,) b January
10, 1828, m Mary E. Goodman. No issue.
5, Jesse Lewis, s of J. Frank, (b June 20,
1829,) m Frances Dunkum, and had issue :
William, Jesse, Lewis, Rosa Lee, Harry L.,
Frances Alice. 6, Ann Elizabeth, dau. of
J. Frank, b August 16, 1831, m Jas. ² D.
Goodman, and had issue, Mary Mildred,
who m James W. Garnett, Culpeper, and
has issue, one child.

7, Mary Catherine, dau. of J. Frank, b
August 16, 1837, m and had issue, John
Thomas, Mathew Fry, Mary Frances,
Martha Mildred, Lizzie Lovell and Jennie.

VII.—John, (s of Rev. Henry,) b June 1775, d
April, 1844,) m Miss Haywood of Culpeper,
Issue : 1, William, m Miss Jones, Ala-
bama, and his widow married Gen. Sam
Lewis, Va. 2, George m Anna Jones,
Alabama. 3, Thomas, d. s. p. 4, Austin, m
Miss Sweet, Alabama. 5, Budd H., m
Miss Waters. 6, Joshua Divers, d. s. p.
7, Elizabeth T., m Dr. Archie Strother,
Bath Co. Va., No issue. 8, Susan, m
Hugh Minor, Albemarle.

?X.—Wesley, (s of Rev. Henry,) b March 25,
1779, d 1823. m Sukey, (b 1778,) dau. of
Hugh Walker. Issue : 1, Eliza, m Geo. W

Clarke of Madison, and had issue, 1, Susan
m W. D. Tatum, who left one son, William
H., 2, Sarah, *m* Wm. H. Benton of Lou-
doun city, and had issue: William, Edward,
Mary and Clara. 3, Mary C. *m* John S.
Walker of Madison. 4, Anna E. *m* Philip
Edge, (Albemarle,) and had issue, Mary H.
Anna B., Grace and Rosalie Fry.

II, Clara H., (*dau.* of Wesley,) *m* Dr. Wm. T.
Banks, Madison, and has issue, 1, William
m Mary Willis and had issue; Ida, who *m*
Wm. H. Early, James W., *m* Shippa Bur-
nett, Sarah, Mollie, *m* Wm. H Browne,
Henry, John, Fanny B. 2, Sophie Banks,
m Mr. Allen, (Powhattan.) 3, Dr. J. L.
Banks, who *m* 1st, Miss Hobson, *m* 2d,
Bettie Carson. Issue, Minnie. 4, Clara, *m*
James B. Willis.

III.—Francis Thornton (*s* of Wesley,) *b* August
12, 1803, *m* 1st Miss White and had issue;
Leah, who *m* Dr. Angus Rucker, leaving
issue in Missouri, Clara Bell. Francis
Thornton, *m* 2d, Sarah Carpenter, and had
issue, 1, James Henry, Clerk of Lee County,
Texas, who *m* and has two daughters. 2,
John W., *m* Nannie, *dau.* of Dr. Alfred
Taliaferro, Culpeper. Issue, Nannie. 3,
Capt. Wm. O. Fry, (C. S. A.,) Lawyer,
(Charlottesville,) and Delegate to General
Assembly from Albemarle, 1862–5 : *m* Lucy

T. Saunders of Tennessee. 4, Thomas V.
(C. S. A.,) Delegate from Madison, 1877-8,
m Octavia, *dau.* of Parker Ayler; issue,
Roy, Lucien, and Harry. 5: Hugh N.
(C. S. A.,) *m* Etta Hill; issue, Fitzhugh,
Frank, Etta.

IV.—Joshua, *s* of Wesley, *d. s. p.*

V.—Catherine, (*dau.* of Wesley,) *m* Thos. White.
Issue: 1, Thomas V., Galveston, Texas.
2, Rufus C. Paducah, Ky. 3, Hugh L., St.
Louis, Mo.; (name of wife not known.) 4,
Octavia, *m* Mr. Booker, Miami, Mo. 5,
Daniel, (Michigan.) 6, Kate, *m* Mr. Mc-
Daniel.

VI.—Martha, *dau* of Wesley, *d. s. p.*

Wesley Fry, *m* 2d, (January 16, 1717,) Sophie,
dau. of Dr. Peter Leflet. She was born in
Paris, France, (1790,) Issue.

VII.—1, Henry, *m* Martha Webb: *m* 2d, Bell
Burnett. Issue: Wesley, Henry, Fanny,
John W., Lizzie.

VIII.—Sarah, *b* April 23, 1821, *m* Wm. T. Nichol.

IX.—Wm. D. Fry, *m* Catherine, *dau.* of Belville
Fry. Issue: Lucy Leigh, Chas. Budd, and
Hugh N. Meriwether.

X.—Rosalie, *m* Henry White, Waco, Texas.
Issue: Sophie, (Mrs. Smith,) Rosalie, Mrs.
Sturgis, Fry.

XI.—Cornelia, (Mrs. Webb).

XII.—Lizzie.

XII.—Virginia, *m* J. E. Bradford.

Thornton, (*s* of Rev. Henry), *b* November 21, 1786, *d* November 26, 1823, *m* November 21, 1811. Eliza R., *b* January 14, 1794, *dau.* of Hon. Philip Rootes Thompson, member of Congress from Culpeper, (1801–1807). Issue : three children, died infants.

4. Cornelia, *b* August 25, 1817., *m* Jno. Lyddall Bacon, President of State Bank, Richmond Va., and Vestryman of Monumental and St. Paul's Churches for forty years. Issue :

1, Richard Wilmer; 2. Charles Lyddall; 3, Margaret Cunningham; 4, Susan Lee. 5, Francis Thornton, M. D., Quinnemont, W. Va., *b* September 2, 1819. *m* Sarah, *dau.* of Dr. Frank Boykin, Isle of Wight, Va. Issue : Francis Burkitt. 6, General Burkitt Davenport Fry, C. S. A., *b* June 24, 1822., *m* Martha A. Micou, Augusta, Ga. These two streams meet again after four generations.

To return to the children of Col. Joshua and Mary (Micou) Fry : Martha (*b* May 18, 1740,) *m* John, *s* of Dr. George Nicholas, (Immigrant to Va.) He

(John), was the progenitor of the Nicholas of the 7 Islands, James' River. His seat is marked in Fry's map, in the S side of the Fluvanna, (James') River, near Slate River, in what was then Albemarle Co., (now Buckingham.) He was clerk of Albemarle,— the Court House then, having been at or near Scott- ville. His son John C. went to school to Wm. Fon- taine, at Union Hill, 1775. He (the son,) *m* Miss Carter of Williamsburg, and one of their daughters is now an inmate of St. Paul's Church Home in Richmond. There were other sons of John and Martha Fry., viz : Robert Carter, George and Joshua Fry Nicholas. The two first have descend- ants in Buckingham, but the writer has no informa- tion as to these, except that a Robert Nicholas owned the Virginia mills. Joshua Fry Nicholas moved to Kentucky, and one of his daughters *m* a Brown, another *m* a Morton, and a third *m* Winn, and Mrs. Lizzie Simpson Winn in or near Winchester, Ky., is the only representative of their family known to the writer. Dr. Geo. Gilmer in a letter to Col. Wm. Cabell, Sr.; as I (learn from Mr. Alex. Brown), dated June 5, 1790, says : "Col. Jno. Nicholas carried me in his chariot to 7 Islands, to see his father con- fined with a severe fit of the gout."

Dr. Geo. Nicholas (the first,) had other sons be- sides the foregoing John of 7 Islands, viz : Robert Carter and George. Robert Carter, Colonial Treasurer, (see Grigsby's Convention of 1776); *m* *dau.* of Wilson Cary, (Hampton), and had issue :

1. George, Gov. of Kentucky, who left distin-
   guished descendants. 2, Lewis. 3, John, *m*
   Miss Rose, and has descendants in Geneva,
   N. Y 4, Wilson Cary, U. S. Senator, *m* Miss
   Smith and had issue : 1, Robert Carter, U.
   S. Senator, La., and John, U. S. N. 3,
   Jane, *m* Thos. Jefferson Randolph. 4,
   Elizabeth *m* Edmund Randolph, Secretary
   of State, etc., one of whose daughters *m*
   Bennett Taylor, father of Jno. C. R. Tay-
   lor and of Charlotte Taylor, who *m* Mon-
   cure Robinson of Philadelphia. 5, Anne, *m*
   J. H. Norton, and had issue : 1, Courtnay
   m 1st, Warner Lewis ; *m* 2d, Landon Car-
   ter, of P. William ; 2, Ann, *m* Gen. Arm-
   stead ; 3, Rev. J. H. Norton, who *m* Miss
   Galt, of N. Y., and had issue : 1, Rev. John
   Nicholas Norton, D. D., of Louisville ; 2,
   Rev. George Hatley Norton, D. D., of
   Alexandria ; 3, Robert Carter Norton, Ohio.
Judge Philip Norborne Nicholas of Richmond,
   Va., (*s* of Wilson Cary,) *m* Maria Byrd of
   Westover, and left issue : Philip Cary, Liz-
   zie Byrd and Sidney.
William, *s* of Col. Joshua Fry, *b* 1743, *d* single.
Margaret, *dau.* of Col. Joshua Fry, *b* May 15,
1741, *m* a Mr. Scott, probably of the family who
founded Scottsville, but the writer after using due dil-
igence has not been able to learn anything of their de-
scendants authentic enough to warrant publication.

FAMILY OF DR. THOMAS WALKER, CASTLE HILL.

Dr. Walker's ancestors (it is believed) came from Staffordshire, England. Capt. Thomas Walker was Burgess from Gloucester Co., Va., 1662. In 1666 he is called Major Thomas Walker, in the list of Bur. gesses. Titles were strictly applied because they meant something in those days. His grandson Thomas Walker, lived in King and Queen, and married there in 1707. He was the father of D$_r$. Thomas Walker of Castle Hill, Albemarle Co., who was born January 25, 1714, and died November 9th, 1794. He is believed to have been the first white man who explored Kentucky. He was Commissary General of Virginia troops in Braddock's war; Member of House of Burgesses; of the Virginia Convention of 1775; Commissioner to treat with the Indians after their defeat by Andrew Lewis, Commissioner to run boundary line between Virginia and North Carolina, known as Walker's line, and he was the guardian of Thomas Jefferson. He married in 1741, the widow of Nicholas Meriwether, whose maiden name was Mildred Thornton. Issue :

1. Mary, *b* July 24th, 1742, *m* Nicholas Lewis of Albemarle.

2. Col. John Walker of Belvoir, *b* February 13th, 1744; confidential A. D. C. to Washington ; M. C. and Senator, U. S. *m* Elizabeth, *dau,* of Bernard Moore and *g*-daughter of Gov. Spotswood.

NOTE—N. Lewis was Surveyor of Albemarle and was succeeded in 1773, by Thomas Jefferson.

The following is a copy of the correspondence between Dr. Thomas Walker and B. Moore, on the occasion, from the originals now before me.

May 27th, 1764.

Dear Sir:—My son, Mr. John Walker, having informed me of his intention to pay his addresses to your daughter, Elizabeth, if he should be agreeable to yourself, lady and daughter, it may not be amiss to inform you what I feel myself able to afford for their support, in case of an union. My affairs are in an uncertain state; but I will promise one thousand pounds to be paid in 1766; and the further sum of two thousand pounds I promised to give him, but the uncertainty of my present affairs prevents my fixing on a time of payment:—the above sums are all to be in money or lands and other effects at the option of my said son, John Walker.

I am, sir, your humble servant,

THOMAS WALKER.

COL. BERNARD MOORE, ESQ.
IN KING WILLIAM.

May 28th, 1764.

Dear Sir:—Your son, Mr. John Walker, applied to me for leave to make his addresses to my daughter Elizabeth. I gave him leave, and told him at the same time that my affairs were in such a state that it was not in my power to pay him all the money this year that I intended to give my daughter, provided he succeeded; but would give him five hundred pounds next spring, and five hundred pounds more as soon after as I could raise or get the money; which sums you may depend, I will most punctually pay to him.

I am, sir, your obedient servant,

BERNARD MOORE.

III.—Susan, (often called Sukie), *b* December 14th, 1746, who *m* Henry, often called Harry Fry, then Deputy Clerk. of Albemarle.

IV.—Thomas, *b* March 17th, 174⅜, *m dau.* of Thos. Hoops, of Carlisle, Pa., who educated Benj. West, the painter. One of Thomas Walker's daughters, Maria Barclay, *m* Richard Duke, of Albemarle Co., (descendant of Sir Edward Duke, Baronet), and by him had Col. Richard Thomas Duke, C. S. A., M. C., and now Delegate of Albemarle. One of Thomas Walker's *g*-sons is Gen. Reuben Lindsay Walker, C. S. A.

V.—Lucy, *b* May 5th, 1751, *m* Dr. Geo. Gilmer of Pen Park, Albemarle, the father of Francis Walker Gilmer, first Professor of Law, University, Va., Author and Scholar ; and of Mildred, wife of Wm. Wirt, Attorney-General, U. S., and *g*-father of Thos. Walker Gilmer, Governor of Virginia, and Secretary of the U. S. Navy.

VI.—Elizabeth, *b* August 1, 1753, *m* Rev. Matthew Maury, Fredericksville Parish, Va.

VII.—Mildred, *b* June 5th, 1755, *m* Joseph Hornsby. No issue.

NOTE.—Mildred Gregory, the grand-mother of both of Dr. Thomas Walkers' wives was the god-mother of General Washington.

VIII.—Sarah, *b* March 28, 1785, *m* Col. Reuben Lindsay.

IX.—Martha, *b* May 2, 1760, *m* Geo. Divers of Farmington, Albemarle.

X.—Reuben, *d* infant.

XI.— Col. Francis Walker, residuary legatee of Dr. Thomas Walker, *b* June, 1764, *d* 1806 : M. C. from Albemarle and Orange counties Virginia. 1792—95.

XII.—Peachy, *b* February 6, 1767, *m* Joshua Fry, Danville, Ky.

Dr. Thomas Walker *m* 2d, Elizabeth Thornton, a double first cousin to his first wife, and both one remove from first cousins to Gen. Washington, thus : Mildred Washington, sister of Augustine, father of Gen. Washington, *m* Roger Gregory, and had by him, three *daus.* viz., Frances, Elizabeth and Mildred Frances *m* Col. Francis Thornton, and had issue, Mildred and Elizabeth ; of these Mildred *m* as 2d wife, Col. Sam'l Washington, the brother of Gen. Washington, and Elizabeth *m* as 2d wife, Dr. Thos. Walker.

Mildred Gregory *m* Col. John Thornton, (brother of Francis), and their *dau.* Elizabeth *m* (as 1st wife) Dr. Thomas Walker

Elizabeth Gregory *m* Reuben Thornton.

Col Francis Walker, youngest *s* of Dr. Thomas Walker, *m* 1798, Jane Byrd, *dau.* of Col. Hugh Nelson, (who was the son of President Wm. Nelson) and Judith Page, (who was the daughter of John

Page of North End, Glocester Co. Va., member
of the Kings council and uncle of Gov. Page.

Judith Page's mother was Jane Byrd of Westover.

Col. Francis Walker, left two daughters, 1st, Jane
Frances, *b* 1799, who *m* 1815, Dr. Mann Page ; issue :
Maria M.; Ella; Frances W. *m* Anna Cheesem,
N. Y., Jno. Cary ; Frederic W. *m* Ann Merewether ;
Jane W.; Maria ; Charlotte N.; Wm. Wilmer ;
Thomas W. *m* Nannie Morris. Dr. R. C. M. Page
m Mrs. Winslow, N. Y.

2d. Judith Page, *b* March 1802, *m* Hon. Wm. Cabell
Rives, to whose memory a Tablet has been erected
in his Parish Church, with the following elegant inscription :

IN MEMORY

OF

One of the Founders of this Church ;

WILLIAM CABELL RIVES, LL.D.,

STATESMAN, DIPLOMATIST, HISTORIAN.

Born 4th May, 1793,
Died 25th April, 1868.

Uniting a clear and capacious intellect,
A courageous and generous temper,
With sound learning
And commanding eloquence :
He won a distinguished place among the foremost men
Whom Virginia has consecrated
To the service of the country,
While he added lustre to his talents,
By the purity and dignity of his public career,
And adorned his private life
With all the virtues
Which can grace the character of Husband,
Father, Friend and Christian.

" Blessed are the dead which die in the Lord. '

The issue of Wm. C. Rives and Judith Page Rives.

1. Francis Robert, *m* Matilda A. only child of George Barclay, N. Y.

2. Wm. Cabell, *m* Grace, *dau.* of David Sears, Boston, Mass.

3. Alfred Landon, graduate Virginia Military Institute and of the Ponts et Chaussées, Paris, and is now Chief Engineer of Ohio and Mobile R. R. Co., *m* Sadie, *dau.* of James B. McMurdo, Richmond, Va., and *grand dau.* of Bishop Richard Channing Moore.

4. Amelia Louise, *m* Henry Sigourney, Boston, Mass., both perished at sea.

5. Ella.

NOTE.—By the mother, (Au Freré), Mrs. Francis Rives is descended from Sir Simon Lockhart, who accompanied Douglas to the holy land with the heart of King Robert the Bruce.

George Barclay was the grandson of the Rev. Henry Barclay, Rector of Trinity Church, N. Y., and a kinsman of Robert, author of the famous "Apology for the Quakers."

THE MAURYS.

The intermarriages between the Maury's and Fry's
suggests the reproduction of some branches of the
Maury Tree. That tree which is delineated upon
the printed chart of the Fontaine and Maury families was too fruitful to be appended to any other
family. They are descended from John De La Fontaine, the renowned martyr of 1563. Several branches of the stock will be found in the foregoing census interlocked with the Fry's.

Mary Anne, *great grand dau.* of the martyr *m* 1716,
in Dublin, Matthew Maury, and migrated to Virginia
1718. He *d* in 1752. She *d* 1755, leaving children
of whom the eldest, Rev. James Maury, *b* 1717, *d*
1769. When he went to England for ordination
Commissary Blair, of Va., gave him the following
credentials to the Bishop of London:

WILLIAMSBURG, February 19, 1741-2

MY LORD :—This comes by an ingenious young
man, Mr. James Maury, who though born of French
parents, has lived with them in this county of Va.,
since he was a very young child. He has been educated at our college and gave a bright example of
diligence in his studies and of good behavior in his
morals. He has made good proficiency in the study
of Latin and Greek authors, and has read some sys-
tems of philosophy and divinity. I confess as to
this last I could wish he had spent more time in it
before he had presented himself for Holy Orders,
that his judgment might be better settled in the
serious study of the Holy Scriptures and other books
both of practical and polemical Divinity. But his

friends have pushed him on too fast. He looks, too, much younger than he is, being of a brood that are of low stature.

He will be, by the time this comes to your Lordship's hands, about 24 years, having been born about the 1st April, 1718. I doubt not your Lordship encouraging our Virginia students. It is a great advantage that one have them from their infancy. They generally prove very solid good men.

My time here must be very short, being in my 87th year.

JAS. BLAIR.

We have seen that he *m* Miss Walker and was Rector of Fredericksville Parish and had 12 children, of whom the eldest was Rev. Matthew Maury, who *m* Elizabeth, *dau.* of Dr. Thomas Walker, and succeeded his father as Rector of Fredericksville Parish, and had 10 children, several of whom intermarried with the Fry's, as did some of their descendants, and therefore need not be re-produced here.

But fragmentary as this notice is, I cannot pass by one of the descendants of Rev. James Maury, who was the greatest man of the name and lineage, viz., the late Captain Matthew Fontaine Maury, U. S. and C. S. N., who was the son of Richard Maury and Diana Minor, and who *m* Anne, *dau.* of Dabney Herndon, of Fredericksburg, Va. He was *b* 14 January, 1806, and *d* February, 1873—he became midshipman U. S. N. 1825 ; Lieutenant, 1837. Being disabled for active service by having a leg broken in an overturned stage in Ohio, he spent several years in Fredericksburg, in study, and in writing in the

S. L. Messenger, a series of articles which wrought a revolution in the Navy department, which led to the Naval Academy, the Memphis Navy Yard and the general warehousing system. In the meantime he had the special thanks of Illinois, for his papers on the enlargement of the Illinois and Michigan Canal. In 1842, he was made Superintendant of the Depot of Charts and instruments in Washington, which, under his inspiration chiefly, became the National Observatory, and the world centre of Hydrographic science. Here he made his renowned current charts and sailing directions, and wrote his " Physical Geography of the Sea," pronounced by Baron Humboldt a " New Science." Here he suggested the conference of Maritime Nations at Brussels, to secure co-operation in observations and researches at sea. The leading powers of Europe showered honors upon him. France gave him two gold medals and tendered the Insignia of the Legion of Honor. Austria presented her great gold medal of Science. Prussia the same, and added at the special request of Humboldt, the Cosmos medal. Russia tendered the orders of St. Anne. Denmark gave that of the Dannebrog. Portugal that of the Tower and Sword. Mexico gave her Golden Eagle and the Order of our Lady of Guadeloupe. Gold medals were struck in his honor by Norway, Sweden, Sardinia, Holland and Bremen, and the Pope of Rome, among other honors, sent him all the medals granted during his Pontificate.

Mr. Tyler wished to put him at the head of the Navy Department, and though but a young Lieutenant, the place of Chief Hydrographer of the Southern Exploring Expedition was offered him. He was (I believe) the first to advocate the little ship and big-gun theory so verified by experience in the late war, and also the substitution of open batteries and earthworks for case-mated forts.

The French Emperor consulted him about the Nicaragua ship canal, and was determined by his advice that it was not expedient for France to undertake it.

The Academies of Science of Paris, Berlin, Brussels, and St. Petersburg, elected him a member of these, and Cambridge, (England), conferred upon him the degree of LL.D.

When Virginia seceded he offered his services and was made Captain and member of Governors Advisory Council, the first act of which was the recommendation of R. E. Lee, as Commander of the Army of Va. When Virginia joined the Confederacy he became its officer.

When it was known in Europe that he had left the U. S. N. and the Observatory, France and Russia invited him to become their guest with every provision for his comfort and studies. He replied that his first duty was to Virginia. He gave much attention to electrical torpedoes in the beginning of the war, and if the Confederacy had had the means of carrying out his plans it is probable that no Southern port would have been entered. When in London, after the war, he instructed committees of the armies and navies of Continental Governments in this formidable mode of defence. In 1862, he was sent on a special mission to England, where he remained until 1865. He was then persuaded by Napoleon and Maximillian to make his home in Mexico, and was appointed Honorary Counsellor of State, a member of the Cabinet and Imperial Commissioner of Emigration.

Before Maximillian's death he was sent on a special mission to Europe, where he remained till 1868, preparing his school Geographies. Being elected Professor of Physics at Virginia Military Institute, he declined the charge of the Imperial Observatory at Paris, and returned to Virginia, where he devoted himself chiefly to the study of the resources of Virginia, and also to perfecting a combined system of crop reports and weather forecasts, for the benefit of the farmer, as his combined observations at sea had been for the benefit of the sailor.

These weather forecasts now so famous at Washington, were urged by Maury upon public consideration in 1854.

But his crowning honor is that science confirmed his faith in his Bible, and that he died as he had lived, a devout Christian. His last words being,

"ALL IS WELL."

The proceedings of the Academic Board of the Virginia Military Institute, on the occasion of his death, is a beautiful tribute to his memory.

GREGORY, LEWIS, WILLIS, AND WASHINGTON FAMILIES.

Mrs. Mildred Gregory was married three times. She *m* 1st, a Lewis ; *m* 2d, Roger Gregory, by whom she had three *daus.* as we have seen. Her third husband was Col. Harry Willis of Fredericksburg, whom Col. Byrd (1736), called the top-man of the place. She named her son by Willis, Lewis, in compliment to her 1st husband. He was a school-mate of Gen'l Washington, being his junior by two years. He said that while the other boys were playing "bandy," George was behind the door cyphering. He remembered but one instance of youthful ebullition in George, and that was "romping with one of the larger girls, which made quite a sensation among the other lads." Col. Lewis Willis was the father of the late Byrd C. Willis, of Willis Hill, (who *m* the *dau.* of George Lewis of Marmion). He was an inimitable humorist, and in some family reminiscences of his, now before me, he tells an anecdote of his *g*-father and *g*-mother (Mrs. Gregory), viz : When his *g*-father lost his former wife, Mrs. Gregory, then a widow, wept so much, for her cousin, that when asked for an explanation, she replied, that she knew old Harry Willis would come after her. And he did, and though repulsed, he besieged her until she surrendered, and he married her in two months after the death of his wife. Byrd C. Willis was the father of Mrs. Achille Murat and Mrs. Gen'l. Thos Botts, of

Murat, and Lewis Willis, and of the late Col. George Willis of Wood Park, who m Miss Smith of Fredericksburg, now a widow at Wood Park, Orange county, Va. Byrd Willis' family reminiscences and traditions would, if printed, be an interesting contribution to Virginia genealogies.

A Lewis genealogy too is a desideratum. I have some materials for it, but they are too imperfect for publication. I subjoin the family record of Col. Fielding Lewis of Fredericksburg, (Merchant, Burgess, Vestryman, &c.) This record is the more valuable from its preserving the names of Godfathers and Godmothers, who in this case are generally historic people.

Fielding Lewis m 1746, Catherine Washington, (cousin of Gen. Washington.) Issue :

 i, John, b June 22, 1747—his uncle John Lewis and Charles Dick—Godfathers ; Mrs. Mary Washington and Mrs. Lee, Godmothers.

 ii, Frances, b November 25, 1748, Fielding Lewis and George Washington, Godfathers ; Miss Hannah Washington and Mrs. Jackson, Godmothers.

 iii, Warner, b November 29, 1749, his uncle, Mr. Lewis and Capt. B. Seaton, Godfathers; Mrs. Mildred Seaton, Godmother. He d infant.

Mrs. Catherine Lewis d February 1749-50, and Fielding Lewis m 2d, Betty, only sister of George Washington. Issue :

I.—Fielding, *b* February 14, 1751, his uncle Geo. Washington and Robt. Jackson, Godfathers; and Mrs. Mary Washington and Mrs. Frances Thornton, Godmothers.

II.—Augustin, *b* Jan. 22, 1752, his uncle Chas. Lewis and Chas. Washington, Godfathers; his aunt Lucy Lewis and Mrs. Mary Taliaferro, Godmothers.

III.—Warner, *b* June 24, 1755, his uncle, Chas. Washington and Col. John Thornton, Godfathers; Mrs. Mildred Thornton and Mrs. Mary Willis, Godmothers.

IV.—George, *b* March 14, 1757, Chas. Yates and Lewis Willis Godfathers; Mrs. Mary Dick and his mother, Godmothers.

V.—Mary, *b* April 22, 1759, Samuel and Lewis Washington Godfathers; Mrs. Washington and Miss Mary Thornton, Godmothers.

VI.—Charles, *b* October 3, 1760, Col. George Washington and Roger Dixon, Godfathers; Mrs. Martha Washington and Mrs. Lucy Dixon, Godmothers.

VII.—Samuel, *b* May 14, 1763, Rev. Musgrave Dawson and Joseph Jones, Godfathers; Mrs. Dawson and Mrs. Jones, Godmothers.

VIII.—Bettie, *b* February 23, 1765, Rev. Mr. Kice and Warner Washington, Godfathers; Mrs. Harriet Washington and Miss Frances Lewis, Godmothers.

IX.—Lawrence, *b* April 4, 1767, Chas. Washington and Francis Thornton, Godfathers; Mrs. Mary Dick, Godmother.

X.—Robert, *b* June 25, 1769, George Thornton and Peter Marye, Godfathers; Miss Mildred Willis and Mrs. Ann Lewis, Godmothers.

XI.—Howell, *b* December 12, 1771, Joseph Jones and James Mercer, Godfathers; Miss Mary and Miss Milly Dick, Godmothers.

DR. JAMES CRAIK,

SURGEON TO COL. FRY'S REGIMENT.

Dr. Craik was born at Orbigland, Scotland, 1730, graduated at Edinburgh, practiced his profession in the W. Indies, and lived in Norfolk, Winchester and Alexandria.

In 1754, he was commissioned as Surgeon in Col. Fry's regiment, and doubtless attended him in his last illness. He was with Washington in the French war, and was present when Washington read the burial service at the grave of Gen'l. Braddock. He was Surgeon-General to the Continental Army in the Revolution, and held other high offices. He was complimented by Act of General Assembly with Washington, Adam Stephen, Woodward and other officers for gallant conduct in the battle of Monongahela, &c.

The name is mis-printed, Craig, in Henning's Statutes. He *m* 1760, Marianne, *dau.* of Col. Chas.

Ewell, (and Sarah, *dau.* of Col. Edwin Conway, and Sarah Ball, his wife, who was half sister of Mary, the mother of Washington. Dr. Craik's wife was a sister of Charles Ewell, the father of Lt. Gen'l Ewell, C. S. A., and also of Dr. Ewell, now President of William and Mary College. One of Dr. Craik's sons, (George Washington), was Gen'l Washington's private Secretary during his second Presidential term.

He *m* Miss Tucker of Alexandria, and was the father of the Rev. James Craik, D.D., Rector of Christ Church, Louisville, Ky. Dr James Craik, Sr., *d* February 6, 1814, in the 84th year of his age, at Vaucluse, Fairfax county, Virginia.

SUPPLEMENT TO FRYS, NICHOLAS, AND SCOTTS.

Thomas Walker, (s of Rev. Henry Fry), m 1st, Mrs. Slaughter, and m 2d, dau. of Abram Maury, and when he moved to Todd Co., Ky. had 3 children, viz.: Wm. Wirt, Susan E. and Frances, (the last by his 2d wife). Wm. Wirt m Mary, dau. of Judge Davidge of Christian Co., and had issue, Frances Wirt, who m her cousin, Jas. H. Gray, now Prof. of Mathematics in Bethel College, Ky., who was the s of Thos. W. Gray and Susan E., aforesaid dau. of Thos. Walker Fry. The dau. of Thos. W. Fry by his 2d wife, (Miss Maury), was reared by Mrs. Betsy Vass, of Fredericksburg, Va., she returned to Ky., and married there.

Joshua Fry Nicholas, (s of Jno. Nicholas and Martha, dau. of Col. Joshua Fry) m Miss Marks (a niece of Thos. Jefferson), and had issue, 1, Martha Fry, who m Philip B. Winn, (a native of Va.,) g-father of Mrs. Lizzie Simpson Winn of Winchester Ky., 2, Eliza, (Mrs. Martin), 3, Nancy, (Mrs. Brown) 4, Maria,? (Mrs. Traver), 5, Sophy, (Mrs. Morse, 6, George, 7, Dr. Wilson Cary, 8, Robt. Carter, 9, John.

Margaret, (dau. of Col. Joshua Fry), m Mr. Scott, of Scottville, Albemarle, Va., and had issue, 1, Charles, 2, Daniel, and another who m his cousin a dau. of John Nicholas, and had issue, one son, John Scott, who was reared by his aunt Betsy Nicholas and inherited her estate. He probably has descendants in Virginia.

INTRODUCTION TO THE AUTOBIOGRAPHY OF THE REV. HENRY FRY.

In the winter of 1848–49, I was in the city of Paris, (France). On some festival morning I set out to attend Divine service in the English Chapel in the Rue D'Aguesseau, and passing by the Catholic Church, the Madelaine in the Rue Royale, built after the model of the Parthenon at Athens, I paused for a few moments in the contemplation of its architectural beauties, and in gazing at the imposing ritual of which it was that day the scene. Soon growing weary of the spectacle, I proceeded on my way, and in a few steps my eye was arrested by the words, "La Chapelle Evangelique," (Evangelical Chapel), on the door of an humble edifice, which had the aspect of a school-room. I could not resist the impulse which prompted me to see what was behind these startling words at such a time and place.

Entering, I found a congregation of plain people, on plain benches, listening to a man whose head was silvered with the frosts of half a century or more, telling with simplicity and with seeming godly sincerity, the old, old story of "Jesus and His love."

As soon as the blessing was pronounced I introduced myself to the minister, who told me that he was a "Methodist Preacher." I could not suppress the exclamation of surprise which leaped to my lips at the thought of a Methodist preacher in the heart of Paris, and as it were under the shadow of the

Madelaine. Mr. Cook, (for that was his name) in-formed me that he had divers colleagues itinerating in France.

That good man, with whom I had much pleasing converse, died the death of a martyr, while nursing the sick in a cholera hospital the very next spring.

This incident made a deep impression upon me and it came back vividly to my mind, when in my historical researches, there fell into my hands, a man-uscript autobiography of an old Methodist (local) preacher, who though born in 1738, survived till 1823, and whom I remembered in the days of my child-hood.

" On the blue mountains of my boyhood," whose distance, doubtless lends enchantment to the view, I see his patriarchal form, trembling in limbs and trem-ulous in tone, his head covered with a silken cap, more venerable in the eyes of his neighbors than would have been the triple crown of the Bishop of Rome ; and if the voice of Christians of all creeds could cannon-ize a saint, " old father Fry," as he was called, would have had a high place in the calendar.

So soon as I read this autobiographical frag-ment, I resolved to publish it as an illustration of the man and of the times. I cannot expect the general reader to share in my enthusiasm which is doubtless heightened by associations.

> With the smiles, the tears of boyhood's years,
> The words of love then spoken,
> The eyes that shone, now dimmed and gone,
> The cheerful hearts now broken.

Whilst I am an Episcopalian by baptism, confirmation and ordination in my convictions, and in my tastes, I hope my right hand may "forget its cunning" before I fail to recognize the image of the Saviour of us all by whomsoever it may seem to be reflected. It must not be inferred that by editing this autobiography I concur in all the sayings and doings of its author. I am responsible for nothing but the authenticity of the document, which is written in his own fair hand, and for the saintliness of his character and career. The reader will make his own comments and draw his own conclusions. It has been too much the custom of biographers to interpose their own persons between their subject and their readers, and thus constrain the latter to see the former, not in his own proportion and hues, but in the form and colors transmitted through the author's personal prism. The modern and better method is for the author to put his hero in the foreground, and himself in the background, as when Boswell hid himself behind the colossal form of Dr. Johnson, and let the lion roar in his own tones (in this case it is the lamb) and not in the squeaking treble of the biographer.

Mr. Fry was bred in his boyhood in the Church of England, and tells us he received his first religious impressions from his aunt, a good old Church of England woman. After years of worldly wandering, he was awakened, and it is pleasant to hear him say that he found instruction and comfort in this aunt's letters. The Church of England then was tottering to its fall under the odium of its alliance with the State, whose slave it was and who used it habitually for political ends. The Church of England had no place of worship where he lived. The only place of worship to which he had access was the Baptist, on Crooked Run, and while his social relations with them were kindly and he availed himself of the privilege of public worship with them, he differed with their terms of communion, their type of doctrine, and some of their ways. The Methodist pioneers were then traversing the country and preaching with great earnestness. His heart turned towards them before he had seen one, and he never rested until he found them and cast in his lot with them. I think, from his own account, that he was surprised into preaching without intending it. I can't find his name in the Methodist minutes even as a Local Preacher. I do not think he was formally ordained, for it was not until 1784 that the Methodists separated from the Church of England and administered the sacraments.

And yet he solemnized the rite of martrimony, which would seem to indicate that he had some ministerial authority recognized by the civil laws and which did not disable him from representing his County in the General Assembly of Virginia, as he did in 1785.

The only reference to Mr. Fry which I have been able to find in any Methodist documents, is in Coke's Journal.

After narrating his preaching at New Glasgow, at Bro. Tandy Key's, and lodging in a tavern at a little town called Charleville (Charlotteville), going thence to Martin Key's, (father of Tandy), he says, " I found he (Martin) had shut his door against the preachers, because he had eighty slaves. His youngest son is a local preacher, but his eldest, is a child of Satan like himself. Friday, I preached at Bro. Grymes' ; 24th of May, 1786, I preached at a chapel in a Forest, and here I was met by our valuable friend, Brother Henry Fry ; Sunday, May 22d, I preached in Mr. Fry's great room, which he had built for a ball room, but (I think) before he had used it for a single ball, the Lord caught hold of his heart and turned it into a preaching room. He is a precious man."

It is to be noted that Dr. Coke does not allude to Mr. Fry as being a preacher—he calls him Brother as he had called Tandy Key. It is also remarkable that Mr. Fry does not mention this visit in his autobiography.

84

THE AUTOBIOGRAPHY.

I, (HENRY FRY), was born Oct. 30, 1738, (old stile) of Joshua and Mary Fry, and from the time I was able to discern between good and evil, had good impressions, desires and respect for such whom I looked upon, as qualified and set apart to instruct us in the good and the right way, the *parsons* who were frequently at my fathers.

At about eight years old I was boarded out to school where was little to be seen but pomp and vanity—at fourteen, I was removed to Williamsburg, to live with an uncle and aunt, (as an assistant in his store), here were all things convenient for life and godliness, the old gentleman careful for the present, and my aunt for the future life ; wealth poured in, and the more it increased, the more capacious appeared his desires and assiduity to business, so that my hands were fully employed from morning till night. My aunt appeared as diligent in laying up treasure above—this was her one design, (though not negligent of her domestic concerns,) these must give way. Whenever an opportunity offered, she recommended to all the benefit of laying a good foundation for the world to come—and when any visited her (which was but rare) who could converse with heartfelt knowledge of the operation and fruits of the spirit—how would she enjoy herself ? It appeared to me as if she was like a person cast among a people of a strange country and language, and that when she could perchance meet with one of her own coun-

try, but little would pass between them, but what was
relative to their own country. How frequently have
I heard her lament the inattention and neglect of
others in preparing to meet God. She conceived if
she made a better appearance it might have more
influence and prevail with some to seek the better
country—and from this motive dressed in rich though
not gaudy apparel, but to her mortification, found
her subject but little more regarded in her fine than
common clothing.

But however others disregarded her precepts and
example, they had at times some influence and
wrought *good impressions on my mind.*

I attended family duty, church service and table of
the Lord, which was a curb, and prevented my running into the vices of the town.

My father who brought me to this place, was
chosen to command the Virginia forces raised in
1754, and when he took his leave of me, charged me
to beware of a sect called Free Masons, and come
thou not into their secret (without alledging his reasons), this I received as his dying charge, which in
fact was his last. I saw him no more, he departed
this life on his march to Fort Duquesne, at Fort
Cumberland.

Near the time of my coming of age, I thought it
prudent to go and take care of what my father had
bequeathed me. I left these good old people, and
in the year 1761, a division of Albemarle took place,
and I was solicited to take charge of the Clerk's

office* which introduced me into much business and variety of company.

In June, 1764, I married a daughter of Dr. Thos. Walker, and soon after, purchased and settled on a place, where those who while they resided there, were subject to ague and fever. My friends out of great good will, advised me to keep myself warm with spirits during the season—thereby I should escape the disorder, and being favored with a deal of company whose propensity led that way, induced me to fulfil their instructions. It took such fast hold on me, that in a few years I found the remedy to be worse than the disease, a paralytic disorder seized my nerves, rendering me unfit for business, and though never beastly drunk, was never cool.

From shame of exposing myself, I relinguished my office and retired to my estate in Culpeper, where I was miserably tormented by my besetting sin for several years, lamenting my imprudence, and making frequent resolutions to break therefrom, but in vain—at any time when the heat abated through want of a supply, I was the more miserable, not being able to bear reflection—it appeared as impossible to abstain as to change my nature ; I was miserable with or without it—it seemed like death to quit and as much to continue; what to do I knew not, and others bemoaned my wretched condition. O! that I had

*John C. Nicholas was the Clerk, but Mr. Fry did all the duty. It was common in those days for Clerks to be non-residents, and put their offices in charge of deputies who were practically the Clerks.

never been born—could I be annihilated, or had been " of the meanest class of reptiles."

Mr. Fry passed from one degree to another until his mind and body lost their balance, and his case demanded a Doctor of medicine rather than a Doctor of divinity. So his family Physician thought and took him to his own house, until his mind and body recovered their equilibrium. His picture of his sufferings is very graphic. Sleep departed, and he had, he says, "no rest day nor night." The very air seemed vocal with voices of good and evil spirits striving for the mastery. " My head pained as if it would burst. My bones seemed dislocated, and my bowels curdled together. Billows of wrath passed over me, and out of the belly of Hell, I cried unto God. After a painful process, he believed that his prayers were heard. He told his wife how favored he had been, and that they must have prayers in the family, and that they must begin that day. He thought he should never sin again, and looked upon himself as a peculiar favorite of Heaven, and upon his good wife as one whom God had passed by. But he soon found that old Adam was too strong for young Melancthon, and that the Devil had only transformed himself into an angel of light. He was soon cast down from the mount of happiness to the sides of the pit, sometimes rejoicing in the light and then overwhelmed with darkness. To resume the narrative—

He says : "from that time until I saw the first

Methodist, I was as a little child learning to walk, which would be more often and longer down than upon its feet.

I now visited my neighbors, the B.—(who were the only professors of vital religion within my acquaintance) and they would re-visit me—and I must tell of my travail, &c., whereat they would rejoice, and told me I was converted, which I much doubted, and would question—if I was convicted and born again, why was my peace so broken ? Why was there such a strife within ? Why was my heart so unclean ? I appeared like the house swept of the graces of the spirit and garnished with all manner of concupisence. I thought if I was a new creature, all those things would be done away—that I should have that peace, which the world cannot give or take away—yea, in a word, I thought I should have been perfect. O ! they answered, there is no perfection in this life, you are looking for what none enjoy ; that these things were consistent with all sound conversions, and constituted the warfare which was to continue till death brought us a discharge. So I thought, but could not be satisfied. I now recollected what I had often heard my good old aunt insist upon, respecting the unction from above and the perfect love of God. I regretted I had not taken care of a letter she wrote me soon after I was married, and I said to my wife, if I now had it, I thought I should understand it better than I did, and set more store by it. Whereupon, the dear creature without saying a word, goes to a

drawer and brought it ; wherein I read as follows :
" I wish you and your wife all joy and peace in be-
lieving, so as to abound in hope through the power
of the Holy Ghost; in order thereto, let there be
prayer in your family at least twice a day—so may
you expect others to follow your steps into everlasting happiness, through the strength of the spirit of
Christ, which never faileth them that seek Him. Be
sure, both of you to follow my example of 'searching
the scriptures.' Begin the Bible, and before morning and evening prayer, let at least one chapter be
read. The first of our acquaintance with God is
fear of everlasting punishment, because of conviction
of sin, by the spirit of truth, showing our lost state
by nature—lost in Adam, as being flesh of his flesh—
under sentence of death of body, and through our
own transgression, become subject to the second
death, Rev. 21st ; we are brought to see that we have
no righteousness of our own. The next thing is
Righteousness—even the Lord our righteousness,
who in the gift of faith, hath manifested himself to
us. The language of the soul then is, Thy will be
done."

I was convinced I had not that living faith, the
substance of things hoped for. My desire was to be
pure in heart, but how it was to be accomplished, I
could not comprehend ; but had a sure trust that
whatever the will of God was, would be fulfilled in
me. I lived in the use of all the means in my
power, attended the B. preaching and had the first

opportunity of hearing experiences. When the first two gave in, how they had been exercised and brought to experience the love of God and concluded the Lord had purified their hearts to love and serve him—that they could pray at all times. To my great astonishment, they were rejected, as hypocrites. The third gave in the same, only that he had a desperately wicked heart, and desired to love and serve God. Joy appeared in every countenance and he was received with acclamation amidst a gaping multitude. My conclusion was "God help the christian; if this man is one, I am one." Thence they were taken to the water, after which the Lord's supper was administered. The order of this, I approved, but some things shocked me much, which I could not behold. I turned my back and walked off. In going home, one of the preachers, G. E., overtook me and entered into conversation, and inquired if I had not a mind to cast my lot amongst them. I answered, for communion sake I could readily do it, but observed there were some things held essential and others practised, that I had not faith in and could not reconcile. He enquired, What? In the first place, they would not receive any but those who believed themselves enjoined to go into the water, which I had no faith in, and I objected to the men washing the women's feet. He replied that the men washed the men's feet and the women washed the women's feet. I answered, suppose there is but one woman, must she go unwashed. I constantly attended meetings and went to their association, held in Orange, about the latter end of August, 1774. Great notice was taken of me ; many enquired and rejoiced in my conversion. It was presently whispered, a Methodist preacher was there, and I desired to hear him. It was impressed on my mind that these are the people. I could not recollect that I had ever heard before of such. I importuned some to prevail on him to preach, which he did. His manner and zeal I much approved, but could not understand him ; there was such a mist before my eyes and veil on my heart. However, I could hear the preachers finding fault. He published to preach in the evening at Mr. Grymes, where I was invited to lodge ; it was still the same I could not comprehend his doctrine. He gave notice he was on his way to Philadelphia, and would preach every day if appointments could be made.

I prevailed on the Baptists to appoint for him at their preaching place, near my house. The night before he came, I had no rest, I was so torn with inbred foes, that I was unprepared to hear profitably, but was astonished ; his doctrine was clear and my heart open to receive it. His text was Rev. 8, 1. In the former part of his discourse the B. were filled with comfort, and their joy break forth in praises ; in the latter part, treating on the possibility of falling after conversion and turning aside after Satan, trampling under foot the Son of God, &c., doing despite to the spirit of grace—it was as if he brought strange things to their ears—it proved as water thrown on the fire, their joy was turned into mourning. He assured them their principles and doctrine would lull them to sleep. No sooner was he done than T. A., a preacher, rose up and warned the people to beware of the man and his doctrine, for these were they, who were to deceive the very Elect if possible—Mr. Williams seemed not to regard him, but opened his bag and disposed of many books among the people, and gave notice he would preach at my house in the evening where but few attended. He preached from " Faith is the substance of things hoped for "—his discourse was adapted to my case, and from the ground and bottom of my heart I cried, " Speak Lord, Thy servant heareth," let not the man speak, but if Thou wilt, a gracious word of Thine cans't make me whole ; and so it was, all clouds, doubts and fears were dispelled ; the true light, glorious light, life, power, peace and joy shone in, and filled my ravished soul ; shame at the same time covered me, and I was humbled for having doubted the power and willingness of God, to save to the outermost, and make clean the inside of the vessel, as well as the outside, and out of the fullness of my heart I could not but speak—concluding, every soul in the room shared in the blessing, but soon found my mistake, for addressing my neighbor a B., saying how plain it was—that we should ever doubt the power and willingness of God to save His people from all unrighteousness ; after experiencing His power in bringing us from under the bondage of sin and Satan through the Red Sea, to put us in possession of the Land of Rest. To my astonishment he appeared to be angry.

I visited and attended the meetings of the B, and would urge it upon them to believe that God could create in them new and clean hearts; that His power extended to that which was within, as well as that without; that He could make all glorious within, as well as clothed with wrought gold; that He could save from inward, as well as outward sin; baptise with the Holy Ghost and fire of perfect love; consume our dross and separate our tin; give a single eye and fill the whole body with light; slay the enmity and make of the twain one; creating peace in the holy court of a pure conscience; to which they would answer. You are still out of your senses; you are surely deluded; you have never seen yourself; if you did, you would find yourself desperately wicked, and your righteousness as filthy rags.

I replied: "All this I have seen; but know the Lord, by the inspiration of His Holy Spirit, could cleanse the very thoughts of the heart, and turn the filthy rags into linen, fine and clean; and as He is, so might we be in this world."

"True," said they, "sin only excepted. And if we say we have no sin, we deceive ourselves, and the just falleth seven times a day; and Paul says when he would do good, evil was present with him; and that with his flesh he served the law of sin, and therein dwelt no good thing, and that if I was converted I should see myself in the same light."

To the first I answered : Was not His name called Jesus? For He shall save His people from their sins, etc. 2. If we confess our sins, He is faithful and just to forgive us our sins, and cleanse from all unrighteousness. 3. And as to the just falling seven times a day into sin, there is no such text, and Paul, as a Father in Christ, could not be speaking of himself, but rather personating a Jew, under the law, a person convinced of sin ; the state of a servant or babe in Christ, who, under the first fruits of the Spirit, groans for greater manifestations.

Thus we argued, and thus breathed my longing soul for their salvation. But, O ! astonishing they looked upon me as an enemy ; and, as I attended their meetings, the preachers generally exclaimed against the docrine of Perfection and Salvation from sin. I could not but speak, and as soon as they concluded would confront them before the congregation. At length one of them, T. A., as he stood up, declared he could not preach—a person there was a bar to him. From that time I seldom went among them. For near two years I did not see another Methodist. For that time I was as a speckled bird, a sparrow alone on the house-top. I was tempted. I need not seek after them ; that the Lord, in His good time, would send them, as He had Mr. Williams. My anxiety increased, and there being an association in July, 1776, I went, thinking I should find some there anxious. They always attended such meetings. Immediately on riding up I met

with Mr. Waller, and I inquired of him if there was
a Methodist preacher there. He informed me there
was not. I inquired if any person knew where these
were. One answered: "To-morrow, at Reedy Run
Chapel, there is an appointment for one to preach."
I inquired how far and the way, and passed on.
O! how big was my hope and expectation, and all
the way forming the most pleasing interviews.
That night I lodged at I. Johnston's. I was filled
with love, in contemplating on the pleasing prospect
of mutual affection, and gaining the company of the
preachers, and obtaining preaching at my house,
having prepared a commodious room (originally designed for music and dancing), but now desirious of
dedicating it to the Lord. I was impatient to be at
the Chapel in the morning. Mr. J. I found to be no
friend to the Methodists, and but little acquainted
with their principles. He would not accompany me,
but sent a servant to put me in the way. I got to
the place sometime before the preacher, and when
he came, I approached him with an overflowing
heart and familiarity, solicited his company and
preaching at my house, He asked where I lived,
and if preaching was wanted in my neighborhood.
I told him I thought it was, and said no more, as
the people were waiting to begin worship. O! how
did my soul drink in the Word. I thought him a
wonderful preacher. After attending class-meeting,
I rode seven or eight miles in the evening to another
appointment at Parrots. He appeared rather shy of

me, and much upon the reserve, so that I had but little satisfaction in conversation. All this time the enemy was not idle, suggesting I should have my labor for my pains. When we came to the place the people were waiting. He began worship, and in his sermon dropped some expressions from which I imagined he was tempted to believe I was an imposter, and had only come in to spy out their liberties, which I afterwards found to be the case. No sooner had he concluded, than he took himself away without any notice of me.

I returned home and rested, assured that the Lord would grant the desire of my heart. Sometime after, I heard they had enlarged their circuit, and had an appointment within fifteen miles of my house, where I attended, and found a man according to my wish, P. Gatch, whose spirit and preaching corresponded with the character of a real Methodist. My spirit clove unto him, and the Word preached was as a feast of marrow and fat things to my soul. No ceremony was necessary to introduce an acquaintance. How condescending, how loving and kind; without reserve, I could pour out my soul into his bosom. I entreated for preaching. He told me I might come to his Quarterly Meeting, to be held at such a time, in the Manakin town. I promised I would go—God willing. I went, (though not much short of an hundred miles). Poor, dear man. I found him on a bed of affliction, but rejoicing in God, his Saviour. Stradford, Drumgoole, Glendenning, and several other preachers attended, but I could obtain no promise for preaching. This was in the fall, and the Christmas day following—E. Pride rode up and inquired if there was any appointment for preaching—of which I had no intelligence, though he said two or three notes had been directed to me. We sent out and gathered a few neighbors, and from that time I have had preaching regularly

Bro. Littlejohn was the next, a man skillful in the Word, and a workman that needeth not to be ashamed. The succeeding preachers raised a small society, and appointed me leader. This was a cross indeed, and what I little conceived would be laid upon me, one so unfit, naturally bashful and slow of speech, had never prayed in public or without a form. How did I plead,—but to no purpose. The enemy suggesting, I could never be able to support myself under it ; I must fall a victim to shame and reproach, and be as a block in the way of others to stumble over. The cause lay much at my heart, but I had no prospect of promoting it by exhibiting in public, but thought I would open the way for others. This being formed into a new circuit, I rode about to procure preaching places, as many classes were formed, and our own increased. I was constrained frequently to tell what God done for my soul, and out of the fullness of my heart exhort sinners to flee the wrath to come, and believers to press into the fullness of God Almighty's love. I I was invited to meet a class one Sunday, about ten miles from my house. When I came within sight of the place, I discovered a number of horses tied and an abundance of people in the yard, which caused a damp and chillness to run through me, and I began thus to question : What could bring all these people together ? Surely not to hear me speak and pray with the Society. It was urged, a portion must be given them ; they must not be sent empty away.

After singing and prayer, I opened my Bible at the 4th Chapter of Isaiah, read it and began to speak. A door was opened ; light, liberty and power attended the Word, to the no little astonishment of myself and the people. The enemy suggested : " Did I not tell you you were to be a great preacher ? " I was not ignorant of his device ; and to complete it an old professor, a B,—got me by the hand and says : " Well, you have given us a wonderful sermon,—the true Gospel line." I did not know which way to look. Shame covered me. I felt very small and should have been glad to make my escape, but he held me fast. I was dumb. But a thought ran through my mind to say : " You are too late ; the devil was beforehand with you."

Some time after, I was sent to supply the place of one of the preachers about twenty miles from my house. When I came near, I called upon B. Roberts, whom I knew waited to accompany the preacher. I told him he would not be there, and that I had come to let them know. I got upon the stage, sang, prayed, and gave out : " It is time to seek the Lord," introduced and laid off my subject, stopped to reprove a gentleman who began to regale himself with an apple ; who stood reproved, and put the rest in his pocket. After I had concluded, I heard them on every side say it was as well as if the preacher had been there, and the old gent B. R., knew not how to contain himself—and as he returned, expressed his surprise, saying : It was as well, yea better than if the preacher had been there—to which I answered, "O, let the devil do his own work." Another time I was desired to supply the place of another preacher nearly round the circuit, beginning at the B. B. Church, where there had been a large and lively class, but then squandered, many preferring the honors, pleasures and profits of this world. A text lay upon my mind to speak from, at that place, and that nearly three weeks before I was to set out till I was on my way when another was presented, from which I had spoken with much liberty. It was suggested that if I attempted to speak from the first, I might fall through, that there would be such and such a person there, before whom I should be confounded, and thereby the cause be wounded. I concluded it might be best, and endeavoured to preach from the latter ; but had not proceeded far in my discourse, before I perceived my mistake—my mind was confused and I could not see an inch before my nose. After hobbling through, I was ashamed to look any one in the face. Thereby was I taught not to seek to please men, but God. The next day, I was as much com forted in speaking at the Episcopal Church in Culpeper, Fork Church, as I was cast down the day before.

My labors as a preacher have been chiefly as a substitute, wherein I have been greatly assisted and comforted ; *though I have seen but little fruit, being led chiefly to preach to believers, and enforce the doctrine of sanctification.*

In the year 1785, a "general assessment" having been proposed, and bills published for the perusal of the people who were generally opposed thereto, I was prevailed on to serve as a delegate to the legislature to present their petition against the same.

On the 15th October, I entered Richmond, but knew not where to take up my lodgings, being a stranger to every one who took in boarders. I was recommended to two or three, but upon application, found myself better known than I expected ; and from their excuses conceived they wanted not a Methodist boarder ; and as I passed along the street, I could see the people pointing, and saying to one another, "that was he." Providence cast me in the way of G. T., an old acquaintance, and once a member of society, who enquired if I had provided lodgings. He told me he had taken a convenient room in a private house with two beds, and had till that evening to choose his companion, and would be glad if I would partake with him—for which I was thankful.

The next morning, breakfasting with several others

who lodged in the same house, I was saluted with language very grating to my ears. I ate but little, rose from the table, and retired. Mr. Thompson, who felt more for me than he did for himself, informed Mr. G. S. T., he had hurt that gent's feelings. He inquired how ? Says he, by your swearing. He declared he would not do it again, sought me out and asked pardon, desiring that if at any time I discovered any thing like it inadvertently coming from him, to give him a look and it should be sufficient— and from that time did bridle his tongue in my presence, and a more tender, affectionate man I have not met with, who did not possess vital religion. But it was not the case with Dr. J., a member of the Senate —he was not so conscientious or complaisant, and as we grew acquainted, I often reasoned with him on the impropriety of his conduct—he would acknowledge the same, and one evening as we were by ourselves he confessed he believed the real Christian's to be the only happy life, told me what a religious wife he had, (by the by, I had gathered from his manservant the manner he used her). I answered, " then I make no doubt she is a good wife," and how tenderly he ought to use her. But on the contrary expect he often grieved and wounded her spirit, crossed her in her inclinations and distressed her by encouraging and entertaining company, she could not delight in. He concluded, I might have been " plowing with his man." He then desired I should hear his ideas of what a real Christian should be, which were so just, I could not but ask him how he could rest without possessing it? He answered he had not rest, and left me. At a certain time the conversation turned on the speeches made in the House, I asked him what was the reason I could never hear of his speeches in the Senate, or bearing a message to the House, observing he was fluent enough on any other subject out of the House. He said he could not tell. I thought I could, and told him that if he was at liberty to deck and adorn his discourses with such flowers of rhetoric there, as he did in common conversation, he could be bold enough—he swore he believed I was right.

There was such a number of petitions against the Assessment Bill that none opened in favor of it. What was called the Religious Bill, passed this Session, putting all Societies on an equal footing, though not without great opposition. The Methodist's petition for the gradual abolition of slavery, was presented and voted out with contempt, though on all hands agreed to be equitable, and what must come to pass, but the time was not yet. Some of the principal speakers in favor thereof, a certain gentleman, C. H., prepared and proposed to make a motion to bring in a Bill to limit free denizen and citizenship to those only who should marry, settle and have children, which he read to me, and I took for granted to be designed against those itinerants who come hither turning the world upside down. I asked what those must do who were under a vow of celibacy—of which I believe he was heartily ashamed, for I heard no more of it. In the House some gentlemen would speak for an hour or more together without an oath (for there was a rule against it), but out of the House, would not speak three words without swearing, and plead they could not help it.

My general conduct was to attend from the sitting to the rising which was generally late, dine, and retire to my room, where my companion sometimes would spend the evening, converse upon religious subjects, join in prayer and lament the strange infatuation of himself and many others who were once in society and happy in the Lord—when His candle shone upon their heads, and, however, the case might be with him, he should ever acknowledge the truth of the Methodist doctrine, and would give all the world, if it were with him, as it had been.

Being confined about three months, without much exercise, and living upon high-seasoned diet, I grew more gross and corpulent than usual, after my return I found it irksome to ride and exercise as usual —the consequence thereof was I laid the foundation of a disorder, and by indulgence nourished the same, which in a few months manifested itself in a most violent cholic, which brought on the jaundice, lasted for about ten months and brought me to the gates of death; my family and friends were anxious I should apply to a physician. I assured them none could yield relief, that I did not despise those helps, but was assured they would do me no good, to gratify them I would make a trial, first, of the " Springs," the most able physician attending in these days. He pronounced them ineffectual—to make full proof I stayed three weeks, then must go to his house, where I stayed four more, and regularly observed his directions, taking whatever and everything he could desire, that his shop afforded ; and I believe never was man more studious to do another good ; the disorder baffled his skill and force of all the medicine he gave. I declined daily, and at length I concluded to return home, and blessed be God, was resigned, come life or come death, saying : " Good is the will of the Lord." My assurance being strong, I could say : " O ! death where is thy sting, O ! grave where is thy victory ! " My neighbors and acquaintances visited me, and on preaching days many would attend, expecting every time to be the last they should see me alive ; upon whom I would press the comfort of religion, and when any who had reason to believe had experienced the pardoning love of God, urged them to press after the fullness of faith and perfect love, which purifieth the heart and casteth out fear that hath torment.

A neighboring B. preacher, J. G., came to see me, and when about to take his leave,* I asked him to go to prayer, he gave a pertinent exhortation to those who were present, and in his prayer implored that if it

---

*This was the venerable James Garnett (the elder). It is worthy of note that a great-grandson of this old Baptist preacher and a great-grand-daughter of the old Methodist preacher have lately intermarried, and are living in the same neighborhood where this incident occurred, and they follow the faith of their ancestors—one being a Baptist and the other a Methodist.

was the will of God, to restore me to my health and usefulness again, but says he we believe it is Thy will to take him, and prayed we might all be resigned thereto. These words ran through my mind, "Satan, thou art disappointed of thy hope, and hell shall miss her expectation." My disorder was then at a crisis, that night turned, left me, and I recovered from that time, my flesh returned like a young child's, and I gained strength daily, and at this time being in my 54th year, find myself more hearty, active and strong than I was at 30.

This is the Lord's doing and that my soul knoweth right well. O! may my strength and all that I have and am, be a sacrifice unto the Lord.—AMEN, &c., &c.

The autobiography terminates abruptly at this date, 1792, and I am able to supply a few items from Col. Taylor's Diary—an interesting document to which I have frequently referred in St. Mark's parish, and for an inspection of which, I am indebted to Dr. A. G. Grinnan, a zealous antiquary, to whom I am under obligations.

A few miles below Orange Court House, was an old Episcopal Church called the "Brick Church," which was without a pastor for many years after the Revolution, which dispersed so many of the old clergy of the Church of England, leaving the succession to be transmitted through laymen who were with few exceptions, the only true representatives of the Episcopal Church in the last century. The Rev. Matthew Maury of Albemarle, whose daughter married a son of Mr. Fry, and the Rev. Mr. Belmaine of Winchester, who was paying court to Miss Taylor of this congregation, (both Episcopal ministers) occasionally preached in this church. In the mean time the vestry invited Mr. Waddell, the blind Presbyterian preacher, whom Mr. Wirt has immortalized, to preach at a fixed salary. They also invited the Rev. Henry Fry, who lived some ten miles from it, to officiate for them.

1792. July 1.—Col. Taylor says : " My father and I went to the Brick Church. Mr. Fry, who has been invited by the vestry, read the old church service and preached to about one hundred persons, and gave notice that he should preach a fortnight hence."

May 15.—Heard Mr. Fry preach,

October 14.—Went to church—Mr. Fry read the morning service and Mr. Belmaine preached.

November 11.—Went to church—Mr. Fry performed divine service.

Mr. Fry had been bred in his youth in the Church of England, of which his father was a member and officer, and he had no prejudice against the church service—indeed was never known to speak a word of bitterness against any church.

NOTE.—Under date of May 1, 1791, Col. Taylor says he went to Chinch Hall to Col. Charles Porter's funeral. Mr. Fry and Mr. Tatum preached to a large congregation. Mr. Wirt made his home at Mr. Fry's for several years and had an office in a field, near Locust Dale. Mr. Uriel Mallory, when he bought the farm (where Edward Lightfoot now lives) moved the office and added to it for a dwelling. Edward Lightfoot also lived in it until having gone to decay, it was pulled down. Some of the doors and windows are still preserved.

Mr. Wirt was much at Mr. Fry's and was intimate with his sons. The late Wesley Fry, son of Rev. Henry would tell many anecdotes of Mr. Wirt, who spent much time fishing in the Robertson river and its tributaries. He certainly wrote some comedies there; copies of which were extant, in manuscript, within the memory of persons now living. He began the practice of the law in Culpeper County.

Mr. Wesley Fry said that he was in company with Wirt, when they stopped to hear Mr. Waddell preach the sermon, which Wirt has painted in such picturesque words. Mr. Fry says that Wirt, as they were riding from the church, repeated several times with great feeling, the quotations from Rousseau, which seemed to have made a deep impression on his mind.

Col. Joshua Fry and Peter Jefferson, the father of Thomas Jefferson (President) as we have seen, were intimately associated in their lives and labors. Col. Joshua Fry made him the executor of his last will, and left him his mathematical instruments. This, doubtless, led to the intimacy between their sons. It is not unlikely that Jefferson may have been the occasion of Henry Fry's going to the General Assembly, when the question of a general assessment, etc., (in which he was so much interested), was to be decided. There were once in the possession of the family many letters which passed between Jefferson and Fry, and Wirt and Fry, and between Fry and divers Methodist ministers, but unluckily they were burned in the house of Mr. George Clarke, and in the office of Wm. O. Fry, both of which, with many family papers, were consumed by fire

Two letters of Mr. Jefferson to Mr. Fry, written while he was President of the United States, are extant and will be found below. They have never been in print before to the best of my knowledge and belief.

COPY OF LETTER OF MR. JEFFERSON TO HENRY FRY.

WASHINGTON, May 21, 1804.

DEAR SIR:

When I had the pleasure of seeing you at your own house you expressed a wish to see Priestly's "Corruptions of Christianity;" finding them in a bookstore here on my return, I was happy in the opportunity of gratifying your wish. I meant on my late journey here to have had the pleasure of asking personally your acceptance of them, but the morning I passed you, was so rainy and the necessity so urgent for my being here the next day, that meeting with Mr. Maury in the road, I was glad to leave them with him, to be presented to you on my behalf. The candor and learning of the author renders everything he writes estimable. At the time of his death he had just finished a work which I am anxious to see printed ; it was a comparative view of the morality of Jesus and of the ancient philosophers, but it is not yet committed to the press.

Accept my affectionate salutations and assurance of great esteem.

TH. JEFFERSON.

HENRY FRY, ESQ.

WASHINGTON, June 17, 1804.

DEAR SIR :

I received last night your favor of the 9th inst., and perceived in it those liberal sentiments I have ever believed you to entertain. The work of Dr. Priestly which I sent you has ever been a favorite of mine. I consider the doctrines of Jesus, as delivered by himself, to contain the outlines of the sublimest system of morality that has ever been taught ; but I hold in the most profound detestation and execration the corruptions of it which have been invented by priest-craft and established by king-craft, constituting a conspiracy of church and state against the civil and religious liberties of. mankind. At my request Dr. Priestly wrote a comparative view of the moral doctrines of Jesus and the ancient philosophers which he finished just before his death—it is not yet printed nor have I seen it ; his history of the Church, I believe, is now printed.

I am sorry to learn that your health now continues declining. I suppose it is from a continuation of the visceral complaint you mentioned to me. I then slightly stated to you what I now do more fully. I was taken with such a complaint, the beginning of 1801, it continued on me with more or less violence near two years. Mentioning it to Dr. Eustis, of Boston, he told me there was but one remedy to be relied on, that which had been discovered by the great Sydenham, which was riding a trotting horse. I immediately recollected that every time I had gone home or returned it had been cured for a time.

I got Sydenham's book and observed the numerous instances he mentioned of the radical cure, when everything else had failed by putting his patients on a trotting horse and making them take long journeys. I had not time to take long journeys, but I began to ride regularly 2 or 3 hours every day, it was some time before the effect was sensible, because it takes time to strengthen the bowels, but in about a year I

was completely cured and am now perfectly well.
" Go thou and do likewise."

Accept my affectionate salutations and respect.

TH. JEFFERSON.

HENRY FRY, ESQ.

P.S.—You have time, take therefore a long journey at first.

In 1808, Feb. 19, he lost his wife, who died suddenly of Apoplexy. His record of it is very touching.
She breathed out her soul, he says, into the arms of
her Beloved without a struggle—the heavenly traces
in her face death could not erase. I had often read
of the lovely aspect of death, but regarded it as a
poetic effusion—now I realize it. We have lived together almost 44 years, and she always manifested a
patient, meek and quiet spirit. We have had fifteen
children. We have seen descendants through three
generations, and he added a note, saying: " I have
heard of the fourth generation in Kentucky." Mr.
Fry's health now became more infirm and he
grew very deaf. A venerable lady (now living in
her 84th year) spent much time at his house between 1811 and 1817, and she says she often heard
him sing, but never heard him preach. She also says
that when she told him she was going to be confirmed in the Episcopal Church, by Bishop Moore,
at his first visitation, he expressed much pleasure and
rode to Culpeper Court House—14 miles, to witness
it. In a playful letter written in 1817, to a member
of Mr. Andrew Glassel's family, after an exhortation

to " press toward the mark for the prize," he speaks
of himself as an old Hermit retired to his cell. My
son, Thornton, he says, set out this day for the
Kanawha. I have given up my habitation, my son,
Wesley, having provided a comfortable room for my
accomodation in my last days. He signs his letter,
"Old Father Fry."

Here the old patriarch ended his days at peace
with God and in charity with the world. The following is the obituary that appeared at the time in
the "Central Gazette," a newspaper published at
Charlottesville.

OBITUARY.

Departed this life on Thursday, the 7th inst., at
the house of his son, Wesley Fry, Esq., of Madison,
the Rev. Henry Fry, in the 85th year of his age.
If an unvarying practice of all the virtues and chari-
ties of the heart ever gave a human being such pre-
eminence as that he ought to be held up as an
example and model for others, this distinction is due
to the subject of this notice. He came into the world
encumbered with all its frailties, but with a degree of
firmness and fortitude unsurpassed among men he
put down in succession all his wayward passions as
they rose in rebellion against him, and almost established for himself the character of a saint among men.

Much of his youth was spent in the giddy whirl of
fashion and dissipation, but his superior good sense
taught him the folly of such a course, and after a

series of probation, he assumed, at the age of thirty-seven, the calling of a minister of the Methodist Church, which character distinguished alike for the most devoted piety and for the most disinterested charity and benevolence he maintained unsullied and irreproachable for forty-eight years, and was emphatically styled the "Father of his Church."

While dispensing good in his holy calling, his high character brought him into public life. He had previously been a member of the House of Burgesses from Albemarle, in the memorable era of 1765, when the first difference arose between that body and the Governor of the Colony. He was afterwards Clerk of Albemarle Co., for eight years, and resigned that office through preference for retirement. He was the delegate to the General Assembly from Virginia, from Culpeper in the year 1785, and was mover of the general Emancipation Bill.

In all the relations of husband, father, neighbor and master, his character was of the highest order. He lived in the most rigid conformity to the rules of his church, but was at the same time remarkable for his uniform cheerfulness, vivacity and equanimity of temper.

He sunk to rest with the utmost composure and resignation, fully assured that he was exchanging this for a better world.—*Central Gazette.*

ERRATA.

Page 19, (Note) for *F. R. Herson* read "F. R. Society."

" 20, for *protestatum* read "potestatem."

" 23, (Note) for *a cousin* read "and some of Patrick Henry's."

" 28, four lines from foot of page, for 1760 read "1660."

" 35, (Note) for *Fry Washington* read "Col. Washington,"

" 36. for *Twipin* read "Turpin."

" 40, for *Familas* read "Familiæ,.

" 43, for *Boleo Cook*, read "Boleo Cocke."

www.ingramcontent.com/pod-product-compliance
Lightning Source LLC
Chambersburg PA
CBHW022340020726
47500CB00004B/1205